Table of Contents

30 TALES FROM FOUNDATION
SCP NEW SERIES

--- Rafael Collins---

The SCP Foundation is responsible for locating, trapping, securing, and studying the most terrifying and unfathomable entities ever discovered. They hunt and investigate these strange anomalies, not just of this dimension, but throughout the Multidimensional Universe.

This is the Operations Manual handed to high ranking officials involved in the program. It contains not only the locations of their most top secret facilities; rankings and personnel responsibilities, but also a complete list of all entities currently under SCP authority.

This book contains 30 SCPs. More leaked information will drop soon.

1. SCP-2385 SOMEWHERE IN THE BETWEEN

A worker presses down on the plunger, and moments later a huge explosion rocks the quarry.

When the dust clears, the three quarry workers look on at the pile of rocks that they'll now spend the next days and weeks hauling out.

But then they spot something strange.

There in the newly exposed rock face… is an opening.

The three men stand at the mouth of the previously hidden cave.

They poke their heads inside but it's too dark to see much of anything, except for the fact that the tunnel in the rock stretches on for at least a few meters before it turns and prevents them from seeing any further.

One of the quarry workers slaps his co-worker on the back and dares him to go inside and check it out.

"No way," he tells him as he pulls his hand back from feeling inside the cave wall,

his palm now coated in a sickly slime.

"It's gross in there."

The other two laugh at him.

If they think they're so brave, why don't the two of them go check it out?

The two men stop laughing and look at each other.

Who could have ever foreseen the tables turning on them like this?

But they're not going to back down.

One of the two takes out a flashlight and they step into the cave while the third waits outside.

He watches as the two of them head deeper into the cave, disappearing behind the bend.

Inside the cave, the floor is just like the walls, coated with some kind of substance

making it wet, but also a little sticky.

They half expected the cave to end right around the bend, but now they can see that it continues on.

Not only is there another turn several meters ahead of them, but as they head deeper in they find that there are branching paths too.

This might just be the start of a vast cave system.

There's no telling how far, or how deep, it might go.

They better head back to the entrance before they get lost.

The two turn around to start heading back towards the entrance - but wait, what was that?

They spin around.

It sounded like there was a noise behind them, but there's nothing there, just the empty passageway.

They must be hearing things, they really should get out of here quickly though.

"Come on, let's go."

As they turn to leave though something happens.

With a sickening squishing sound, the walls of the tunnel constrict, closing up between them.

He runs towards the now closed passage and starts slapping at the moist, soft wall, but there's no response.

But then he does hear something… was that a scream?

He's realized something else too, even though his friend had the flashlight, he can still see.

While faint, the walls themselves seem to be producing a small amount of light.

He yells out that he's going to get help and that his friend should hold tight and

not move, he'll get him out here.

He has no idea if he can hear him though.

He starts to slowly make his way back the way he thinks they came, but the cave feels different.

He's taking turns that he doesn't remember making on their short trip.

He should be at the entrance already, and there seem to be more branching paths than there were before.

It's hard to tell in the low light though, maybe he's just confused.

He's hearing noises too… wet, writhing sounds.

He's got to get out of here.

The quarry worker reaches a fork in the tunnel and has no idea which is the right way to go.

He doesn't remember this at all.

He calls down the tunnel but there's no answer to his cries.

He hears more of those wet, slapping sounds behind him though, he's got to keep moving.

Eeny, meeny, miny, moe - the left tunnel it is.

He goes down his chosen path, rounds a corner, and sees… another fork.

What is going on here?

He's got to pick though.

Eeny, meeny, miny - He screams as something leaps out of the tunnel at him.

Outside the cave, the quarry worker is growing nervous.

He's gotten a flashlight of his own and shines it down the tunnel, but he can't

see any more than they could before.

He calls out, asking if they're alright, but he's met only with silence.

He looks around behind him at the empty quarry.

They're the only ones working on the site that day, and if they don't get back to

work soon there's going to be some angry questions about why they spent the day horsing around inside of a cave.

As much as he hates the idea, he's got to go in there and get them out.

He enters the cave and goes around the first bend.

He too notices how oddly sticky and slimy every surface is, but he has to press on,

maybe they were hurt and needed his help.

He rounds another bend and spots something, a pair of legs sticking out from around the next turn.

His friend must really have been hurt.

He runs towards his injured co-worker and kneels down next to him.

It looks like he's passed out on the ground and he tries to shake him awake.

"Are you okay?

"What happened?"

His friend moans a bit, but doesn't even open his eyes.

He moans again, and this time blood starts pouring out of his mouth.

The quarry worker steps back, scared at the sight of his friend's state.

That's when he notices something.

His friend's stomach... it's moving.

He leans in close, he can see bumps swelling and moving around his abdomen.

"Is that...?"

The SCP Foundation soon learned of the troubling reports, and moved quickly to purchase the quarry and the surrounding lands.

Those who had seen or heard rumors about the missing workers were amnesticized and all further access to the area around the quarry was strictly controlled.

The cave itself that had been unearthed was designated SCP-2385, but the Foundation needed to learn just what they were dealing with, so after a research outpost was constructed over the entrance, the investigation into what was happening inside this strange anomalous cavern system could finally begin.

The first to enter the cave is D-11424, a Class D personnel, who is equipped with a shoulder mounted camera, a Ruger LC9 pistol, a machete, and one week's worth of rations,since it was unknown just how vast this cave system may be.

D-11424 proceeds into the cave and immediately reports back the same conditions that the workers had experienced, that the surfaces of the cave were soft, wet, and a little sticky,and also that they seemed to have an almost imperceptible glow.

D-11424 moves deeper into the cave but sees no sign of the missing workers, despite one of their bodies having been reported as being lost relatively close to the entrance.

He's ordered to continue deeper into the cave and radios back that the walls weren't stable.

He would pass by openings in the walls that would seal off once he was past.

On more than one occasion he saw new passages open up as well.

And these didn't appear to be caused by collapses or other geological activity.

The walls seemed like they were alive.

But the walls were the only sign of life he could find.

There was still no evidence of the missing workers or whatever might have gotten them.

But then, after D-11424 rounds a corner, he sees that something is up ahead of him.

It's not one of the workers, it's a creature, and one that looks like nothing he has ever seen before.

The thing crawling on the floor of the cave looks like a giant worm, several feet in length, but with a grotesque, skinless, human head.

D-11424, frightened at the sight of this grotesque creature, turns to run but it's too late.

The worm has spotted him and charges at him immediately, slithering across the wet cave floor at an incredible speed.

D-11424 slips and falls to the ground, his shoulder mounted camera knocked off his body and left and facing a wall, leaving the researchers monitoring the feed with nothing except the sound of his screams.

Once contact was lost with the Class D Personnel, the Foundation decided that due to the presence of hostile creatures within the cave system, that the next exploratory expedition would be undertaken without humans.

The mission was authorized and two months later, a remote controlled drone designated A-47 was sent into the cave.

Just like D-11424 and the quarry workers before saw, its camera captures passageways opening and closing in the living rock walls.

As it progresses deeper, it eventually spots the same worm-like creatures with horrible human faces that look like they've had their skin removed, which have now been designated by the Foundation as SCP-2385-1 entities.

And A-47 soon discovers a surprising fact about these bizarre organisms - they appear that they are being birthed right from the walls of the cave itself.

As A-47 enters one of those largest rooms yet seen in the cave, its camera captures over a dozen 2385-1s growing out of the walls and ceiling in various stages of maturity.

Some of them snap at A-47 as it passes by, trying to attack the drone, but luckily they're unable to reach.

There's larger examples of the worms in the room too, and these ones also differ in

appearance slightly, with a fibrous growth over their eyes.

The researchers assume that these entities are different enough from the smaller versions that they warrant their own classification and are designated as SCP-2385-2 entities.

Luckily for A-47, these larger specimens which can be as large as four meters in length seem much more docile than their smaller counterparts and ignore A-47 as it passes by.

A-47 then learns another shocking piece of information about these disturbing worm-like creatures - they're cannibalistic.

Its camera relays footage back to the research team of a 2385-1 entity feeding on another, smaller one.

It appears that they eat their prey whole after unhinging their grotesque jaws.

The one feeding tries to lash out at A-47 with its tail, but can't reach him with half of another instance in its mouth, and the drone continues deeper into the cave.

Just when A-47 enters the next chamber, a 2385-1 instance growing out of the ceiling drops down right in front of it, leaving no way for the drone to get around it in the narrow section of cave.

A-47 quickly turns around to seek out another path but its camera captures the passage closing in front of it.

A-47 is trapped.

The 2385-1 entity charges towards the remote controlled drone and attacks, biting and slapping it with its powerful tail.

It then attempts to consume it but is unable to ingest the bulky drone and instead leaves the heavily damaged robot for dead, slithering away deeper into the cave.

The battered drone lies immobile on the cave floor for several hours, its camera broadcasting until the last of its battery is finally about to run out.

Just before it stops sending signals back to the research outpost though, it captures something.

The wall next to A-47 opens up and two of the larger SCP-2385-2 entities emerge from the new passageway.

One of them approaches A-47 as the other probes at the wall next to it with its head.

It seems as though the larger of the entities are actually able to form new pathways in the cave, or at least open up doorways between existing ones.

With the last of its battery power, A-47 sends back a truly remarkable sight.

Out of the hole opened by the 2385-2 entity, appears D-11424.

He's dirty, disheveled, sporting a month's worth of beard growth, and brandishing a machete.

The wall opens up from the -2 entity prodding at it and the odd group exits through it.

It's the last thing A-47 transmits back to the Foundation.

Two months later, after several more failed manned missions, there was finally a success.

An SCP-2385-2 instance that had wandered close to the entrance was retrieved from the cave system and brought back to a Foundation research site where a camera was surgically implanted in its head.

The entity, which was designated as Subject Alpha or S-A, was then amnesticized and released back into the 2385 caves, allowing researchers to monitor how it behaved as it traveled through its home environment.

The researchers watched as S-A made its way through the cave system and stopped in another of the rooms filled with young versions of 2385-1.

The larger entity approached several and appeared to nuzzle its face against theirs before moving on, which looked to have a calming effect on the extremely aggressive smaller versions.

As it continues through the tunnels, S-A, sees a group of 2385-1 instances feeding on a deceased 2385-2.

It appears that when 2385-1s are unable to swallow their prey whole, they burrow into the body and consume them from the inside out.

Luckily they are too distracted by their meal to pay any attention so S-A and it is able to pass by.

S-A then runs into two other 2385-2 entities and the three begin traveling through the caves together.

They're soon attacked by a smaller -1, but the group is able to pin the biting and thrashing entity to the ground with their powerful tails, allowing S-A to nuzzle it.

Just like with the ones being birthed from the wall, this seems to calm the creature, but there is another effect as well.

As the 2385-1 entity becomes more docile, the same fibrous growths that can be seen on the larger 2385-2 entities start to grow over its eyes.

Is this how 2385-2s are created?

The group of -2s continues their journey through the tunnels, often stopping to prod at the walls to open new pathways.

It appears that they are searching for something, looking around each new room they enter before moving on.

Eventually they run into something, but it doesn't appear to be what they wanted to find.

They enter a new section of cave, and blocking the path in front of them is the largest SCP-2385-1 entity yet recorded.

It's as big as the -2s at over 7 meters in length and weighing an estimated 400 kilograms.

It appears to be extremely hostile but the -2s seem to instinctively know that the only way forward is to go past this massive -1.

The trio nuzzles their heads together as if they are saying one final goodbye before one of the -2s charges straight ahead.

The -1 attacks and quickly incapacitates it with its powerful tail and snapping jaws.

It begins feeding on the -2, giving S-A and its one remaining companion the time they need to get past.

As the now duo moves past, the other is attacked from a side tunnel by a group of regular sized but ferocious -1s.

S-A can't do anything to help.

It seems to pick up the pace and continues on but as it rounds a corner, it comes face to face with another large -1 instance.

It turns down a side tunnel to avoid it but finds itself in a dead end.

It prods at the wall as the -1 rushes towards it but no new passageways open.

It turns around seemingly resigned to its fate as the -1 begins attacking.

But just then, something else appears in the tunnel coming towards them.

It's D-11424, charging forward with his machete raised in the air, his hair and beard both long and wild.

He begins fighting the large -1 entity, hacking at it with his machete until it finally dies.

With the vicious entity now dead, he kneels down next to S-A and begins stroking its head in a calming manner.

"Hey there, little guy.

"You alright?" he asks as he pets the 2385-2.

"Yea, you're fine.

Get up.

I know where it is, come with me."

S-A struggles from its injuries but is able to follow D-11424 as he leads it through the tunnels, with D-11424 stopping at one point to carve a piece off of the fleshy walls and consume it.

The tunnels eventually open up into a large room that looks similar to the rest of the cave system except there is a huge, glowing orb at its center.

It's a beautiful sphere of warm light that appears to be at least 10 meters in diameter.

"Here we are," the D-Class tells S-A, and motions towards the orb, "it's alright."

S-A nuzzles against D-11424, perhaps one final thank you for saving its life, then instinctually seems to know what to do.

The camera feed shows that it began crawling towards the sphere and after a brief pause, started pushing itself inside.

The camera recorded the brilliant light of the orb engulfing S-A and its implanted camera before the feed finally cut out.

The SCP Foundation would later discover that on that very same day in the city of Elgin, Illinois, a local woman was admitted to the hospital after complaining of abdominal pains.

Doctors performed emergency surgery and found something they did not expect… a micro camera had somehow become embedded inside of her body, which upon later investigations, would be found to bear the same serial number as the one that had been implanted in S-A.

Following this strange event, SCP-2385 which had previously been classified as Euclid, was upgraded to Keter.

An observation site has been built at the quarry and no further human expeditions are allowed inside.

In a bit of good news, some time later, D-11424 finally emerged from the cave system.

He was taken back into SCP Foundation custody and continues engaging in exploratory missions on behalf of the Foundation to this day.

2. GREAT WHITE SHARK WAVE CSP-054-FR BLUE FEAR

A teenaged boy and girl are sitting on surfboards, gently bobbing up and down in the calm ocean water.

This surfing trip didn't turn out nearly as exciting as they had hoped it would, so with no waves in sight and the pair growing bored, they decide to head back to shore.

Just as they're about to start paddling back though, the girl gives one last look and spots the water swelling in the distance.

She calls out for her friend to stop, it's just what they've been waiting for.

Waves are coming in, and big ones too.

They can see that they're going to break at the perfect time, maybe this trip will turn out to be a good one after all.

The boy tells the girl that she can have the first one and she starts paddling to catch it.

She pops up on her board just as the wave breaks, riding it expertly towards the shore as the boy does the same on his own behind her.

They have a great time, riding wave after wave, each one coming in bigger and stronger than the last.

The girl starts to worry though that they might be getting too big and fast.

As the girl finishes surfing another perfect wave she looks back at the boy just in time to see him wipe out on an especially tall one.

He and his board are pulled beneath the water and both disappear under the breaking wave.

She hops off her own board and stands in the waist deep water watching for her friend to emerge, but he doesn't.

She scans the horizon and calls out for him, but there's no sign of her friend.

She's getting worried, he should have surfaced by now.

She doesn't see any sign of him or his board…

What's going on?

"Boo!"

The girl jumps with fright and turns around.

The boy is standing behind her.

But how did he get there?

He tells her that the last wave was a crazy one that must have pulled him and his board under the water towards her.

He's never experienced anything quite like it, but he's fine now, there is nothing
to worry about.

The girl, still trying to catch her breath from the fright gives him a playful punch on the arm and recommends that they call it a day.

The waves are getting stronger and if he was pulled under once, then who knows what would happen if one of them wiped out on an even bigger one.

Besides, the boy looks like he might have hurt himself and the girl points at the small cut on his arm that's starting to bleed.

The boy tells her that it's only a scratch, and insists on catching one more wave before they head home.

He doesn't want to miss this opportunity to ride these great waves when they have the whole ocean to themselves.

He tells her that she can head back if she wants, but he's going out one more time.

The boy starts to paddle back out and the girl reluctantly follows him.

As they wait to catch a wave she tells him that this time he can go first.

She's not going to let him scare her again.

The boy promises, no more surprises, and goes to catch another wave.

The waves are coming faster now and she's able to get on one right behind him.

As she surfs towards the shore, she keeps one eye on the boy.

These waves are tough and she needs to focus, but her attention is drawn towards her friend.

She sees something forming on his wave.

It looks like the water itself is growing out of the crest of the wave and reaching towards the boy.

It looks like... the jaws of a shark!

The girl screams and the boy looks back, straight into the gnashing teeth of the shark reaching out of the waves.

The boy yells in fear and falls, tumbling into the water just underneath the mouth as its jaws snap shut on his board right where he was standing, splintering it into pieces.

The girl can't believe what she's seeing and stumbles on her board.

She catches herself but looks behind her just in time to see the same jaws coming out of the wave towards her.

The boy emerges out of the water carrying his friend onto the nearly empty beach.

He lays her down in the sand, screaming for help as a few beachgoers start running towards them.

No one has any idea what they could possibly do to assist though, both of the girl's legs have been bitten off at the thigh, and it's clear she was dead long before he carried her onto the beach.

...

Bonjour!

Today's file comes from our friends at the French branch of the SCP Foundation.

A frightening and dangerous aquatic anomaly that has been designated SCP-054-FR, but is appropriately also known as...Blue Fear.

SCP-054-FR is an oceanic phenomenon that has been observed occurring in several different regions spread across the world.

In these areas, of which at leave five have been identified, certain waves will display extremely dangerous anomalous activity.

The waves themselves will seem to physically transform, taking on a shape that resembles the mouth and jaws of a Carcharodon carcharias, a species of shark better known to most as the Great White.

The giant shark mouth, which is full of row upon row of razor sharp teeth, will often go unnoticed until it is too late for the unfortunate victim, with the roar of the powerful wave itself covering up much of the sound of the gnashing jaws as it attempts to bite the targeted individual.

The SCP-054-FR phenomenon will only appear on waves in these areas that are at least four meters in height, but a maximum height on which the jaws will manifest has yet to be identified.

Waves carrying the anomalous effect are changed in other ways too. Not only does a terrifying set of carnivorous jaws appear out of the water, but the wave will move faster as well, with SCP-054-FR waves having been measured at rolling three times the speed of normal, non-affected waves.

The frequency of just how often SCP-054-FR will affect waves is not well understood, but what is known, is that waves will speed up when a human or non-aquatic animal is in the water between a wave instance and the coast.

The frequency of 054-FR waves will increase dramatically as well when individuals in the area are at least 250 meters from the coast, and SCP-054-FR does not care which aquatic activities you're engaging in when it spots you that far from shore.

There have been documented cases involving casual swimmers, snorkelers, and divers, but surfers are, for some unknown reason, far and away the most likely victims.

Observations have shown that non-aquatic animals are also at risk of triggering the effect, such as in the case of several seabirds that were seen floating on the water just before an SCP-054-FR wave crashed down on them and the birds vanished, leaving only blood and feathers floating on the surface where they once were.

Even some aquatic vehicles like jet skis and small boats have been observed being attacked by the anomalous shark jaws, though it seems to avoid going after larger vessels.

If more than one person is present in the area that SCP-054-FR is manifesting though, then additional instances of the jaws are able to form, either on the same wave or on multiple different ones in the area.

The injuries caused by SCP-054-FR are very similar to those of a normal, non-anomalous Great White Shark, and the force of the jaws appears to be proportional to the size of the wave itself, with larger waves being more powerful than smaller ones.

Victims of 054-FR attacks have had entire limbs ripped off, others were torn completely in half, while some simply disappeared beneath the wave as it crashed down on top of them and the jaws snapped shut.

The only way to avoid being bitten or swallowed whole is to dive down under the wave before it impacts, but the opportunity to do so is quite rare given the wave's ability to "sneak up" on its victims, and the injuries that are nearly always sustained from an appearance of SCP-054-FR are fatal in 68% of recorded cases.

The SCP Foundation first became aware of SCP-054-FR following multiple reports of shark attacks caused by Great White's emerging out of the waves to attack humans before vanishing back into the water, and the Foundation soon began a series of experiments to try and better understand the anomaly.

The first test performed by Foundation researchers was quite straightforward and involved dumping large quantities of animal blood into the water in an area where SCP-054-FR was reported to have been attacking people.

Just like with a normal shark, the blood seemed to act as a trigger for the anomaly, causing it to manifest in less than two minutes and the researchers watched as the shark jaws tried to bite at the blood as the wave rolled over it.

The test was repeated but this time human blood was used instead.

This also caused instances of SCP-054-FR to appear on the waves, though now they manifested much faster, often showing up less than one minute after the blood was dumped into the water.

It seems that SCP-054-FR has a strong preference for humans or at least their blood, and only a small amount is all that is needed to cause the shark jaws to quickly appear.

Tests involving D-Class personnel have shown that wounded individuals are four times as likely to trigger a manifestation as an uninjured individual, but that there are also ways to limit how often the carnivorous waves will appear.

It seems that lying motionless on the water will significantly reduce how often SCP-054-FR will spawn, and slow body movements will decrease the likelihood of an appearance as well.

Strangely while blood will make the jaws manifest quickly, it is unlikely that it is because SCP-054-FR can "smell" it, since tests that have tried to disguise the smell of both the blood and the human test subjects have all met with failure.

So far, all attempts at damaging the anomaly have also been unsuccessful.

Bullets fired at the shark jaws pass harmly through it, disappearing into the wave as if they were shooting at perfectly normal water.

Given its nature, it seems unlikely that the Foundation will find a way to capture and contain SCP-054-FR, so for the time being all containment efforts have been directed towards keeping humans away from it.

A one kilometer exclusion zone has been established around the five geographic areas where manifestations have been reported and civilians are completely forbidden to access the areas under the guise of there being on-going research into marine mammal life that would be disrupted by the presence of any humans.

Secrecy is of the utmost importance when it comes to SCP-054-FR in order to keep the curious away for their own safety, so any photographic evidence of the anomaly is confiscated and destroyed, and witnesses of an SCP-054-FR attack are given amnestics in order to remove the memory of any anomalous shark attacks from their minds.

The Foundation also engages in an extensive misinformation campaign to debunk any evidence of the anomaly, spreading the idea that any reports of a shark mouth forming on waves are simply hoaxes or misunderstanding of wave dynamics, while attacks are blamed on normal, non-anomalous Great White Sharks.

It is unknown if the five areas the Foundation has contained make up the entirety of the locations where SCP-054-FR can manifest, but Foundation agents continue to monitor reports of shark attacks around the world, and hopefully they will find that they were the result of the regular oceanic super predator, and not the kind that can manifest behind you when you least expect it.

3. GRAMMIE KNOWS SCP-517

"Dance Failed!"

The young woman laughs as her date tries to catch his breath.

The dancing rhythm game was much harder than he anticipated, and he can't help but also laugh at his abysmal score.

He takes her hand and the two continue walking through the arcade.

It's not crowded at all tonight and the two have their choice of games as they bounce between the many pinball tables, driving games, and light gun shooters.

As they finish up a game of air hockey, her date notices something.

It's a door in the back of the arcade that's slightly ajar, the latch and a lock that should be keeping it closed hanging open.

"I wonder what's in there?" he asks.

Broken games?

Maybe ones that let you play without putting in a token.

Or keep spitting out tickets even when you lose?

"Come on!"

The two slip through the cracked door and find themselves in a dark room that doesn't look like anyone has been inside in a while.

There's cobwebs and dust everywhere, but her date was right, it really is filled with broken games!

He motions for her to follow as he checks out an old pinball machine.

He presses the buttons but it remains dark.

He gives it a hard slap and… nothing happens.

How disappointing, they really are just busted old machines.

The two turn to leave, they might get kicked out if anyone finds them messing around in here.

They're back at the door when they both stop and look at each other.

Did they hear something behind them?

The young woman shrieks with fear at the sight of the old woman staring at her.

This time it's her date's turn to laugh at her.

It's just an old fortune teller, nothing to be scared of.

They must have accidentally turned it on.

She didn't notice it before, but the machine which has the words "Grandmother Predictions" written across the top has come to life and the inside is now lit up to reveal the animatronic head and torso of an old woman.

The old woman isn't moving, but her glassy, dead eyes seem like they are staring right at the young woman.

The two look at eachother, unsure of what to do, when without warning, the old woman comes to life.

With the clicking and whirring of gears, the old woman appears to breathe in deeply, opening and closing her mouth as she leans slightly forward and back inside her glass container.

The young woman steps towards the fortune teller as the old woman inside keeps breathing in and out.

But then suddenly, the old woman stops.

There's another loud click as a card appears out of a small slot on the front of the machine.

She looks down at the card, then looks back up to see that the Old Woman is staring at her once again, as if the robotic figure can really, truly see her.

The young woman slowly reaches towards the card as the old woman's gaze stays locked on her.

Her fingers touch the card and at the exact moment she pulls it free, the fortune teller's lights go out and the old woman slumps over.

 "What was that?" her date asks.

She didn't even notice that he is standing next to her now.

He starts to search around the machine looking for something that may have triggered it, as the young woman looks down at the card she pulled from the slot.

Her face changes as she reads it as she goes from a little freaked out, to completely terrified.

 "Hey, look at this" her date says as she quickly slips the card into her pocket.

Her date reaches behind the back of the machine and pulls out a short piece of cord, one end attached to the fortune teller, the other frayed as if it has been cut.

"It's not even plugged in."

"Let's get out of here" she tells him.

She doesn't need to ask him twice and the two leave the room, emerging back into the lights and sounds of the arcade.

Later that night, the two are at the door to the young woman's apartment.

He asks if she's sure she's okay, she's not still scared about that broken machine, is she?

It's probably just battery operated and they switched it on somehow.

The young woman agrees that must be it, and that she's fine, just tired.

She gives him a kiss on the cheek and bids him goodnight before going into her apartment and closing the door.

Inside, the young woman leans against the door.

She takes something out of her pocket and stares at it.

It's the fortune that was dispensed from the machine.

It reads:

You look like you've made some mistakes.

Some things are unforgivable, aren't they?

"No way" she thinks to herself.

"It's just a coincidence."

The young woman walks further into her apartment and picks up a framed photo.

It's a picture of her several years younger, with another girl who looks just like her.

Her sister.

She thinks back to that night.

The night that she'll never forget no matter how hard she tries.

The night she lost her, and lost part of herself too.

She sets the picture back down on the table before looking at the fortune she's still

holding in her other hand.

She crumples the paper in her fist and drops it in the trash before heading to bed.

It's late at night and the young woman is tossing and turning with bad dreams when she suddenly pops up awake.

Did she hear a sound?

She looks around her dim room but nothing looks amiss.

There it is again though, a noise... is it coming from... the closet?

She gets up out of bed and walks towards the closet, one slow step after another.

She reaches towards the closet door, but the moment her fingers touch the knob, the door bursts open.

She screams and falls backwards as multiple arms reach out of the darkness in the closet towards her.

She screams and kicks at the arms as they grab at her, trying to pull her inside.

She fights with all her might as she tries to crawl away from the arms.

She manages to escape their grasp and stands up.

She runs out of the room and towards the front door as the arms follow, reaching out of the closet, growing longer and longer, the sickening sound of bones twisting and snapping as they form new joints to bend around corners.

Her hands reach out for the knob and she grabs it, just as the arms grab onto her.

She's jerked backwards and falls to the floor as the arms drag her down the hallway.

She tries to resist, her fingernails digging into the floorboards as the arms pull her

back into the bedroom.

 "Hello?

Are you awake?"

The woman knocks loudly on the front door.

 "Come on, we have reservations.

You have to get up"

The woman knocks again but still no response.

She checks her watch and with a sigh, takes out a set of keys.

She finds the one she's looking for and unlocks the door.

 "Everyone is waiting for us and I'm going to tell them we're late because of - "

The woman gasps as she opens the door.

She can't believe what she's seeing.

The apartment is a mess.

It looks like a bomb went off.

She looks around but there's no sign of her daughter.

Then she notices the bloody claw marks leading down the hall towards the bedroom.

She runs down the hall, stops in the doorway to the bedroom, and screams.

If you've ever been to an arcade, a midway, or a boardwalk, then you may have encountered a fortune telling machine.

These small booths containing an automaton are great fun as you receive a random card that purports to tell you your future or reveal a secret truth about yourself.

There's nothing to it obviously, it's just a random card you're getting after

all, but the SCP Foundation has a fortune telling machine in its possession that's

both very real, and very dangerous.

SCP-517 as it is known to the Foundation, is a two meter tall, glass and wooden fortune telling machine that contains an mechanical, animatronic facsimile of an elderly woman wearing a white blouse and a blue shawl.

On top of the machine is a panel with the words "Grandmother Predictions" written on it.

Once per hour, the machine will power on if an individual enters what could be considered the elderly woman's field of vision.

She will turn to directly face the person, seeming to stare right at them, before dispensing a fortune card from a slot on the front of the machine, after which it will appear to shut down and cease to function.

It is unknown just how the machine becomes active, seeing as the only cord coming out of the back of the machine appears to have been severed.

The "fortunes" dispensed when the machine comes to life are less a prediction, and more of a veiled threat, and examples of ones received have included:

"Your mother raised you better than that.

I'm sorry, but fair is fair."

"Some people don't know how to be kind.

You'll know soon enough, won't you?" and "People who do terrible things deserve terrible things. You've brought this upon yourself, my dear."

Following an activation of SCP-517, starting at 1:43 AM local time, the same events will always occur.

The individual that was targeted by the machine will find themselves attacked by a number of entities which have been designated as SCP-517-01.

These entities are long, multi-jointed arms that emanate from a location nearby the individual.

The exact number that appears will vary, but there usually seems to be between ten and thirty-six.

The arms will appear from a single location that's often a low, cramped, and dark space like a closet, basement, or under a bed.

The arms will reach out from this area and try to grab the individual before dragging them back to the location where they manifested.

They appear to be able to stretch indefinitely, growing as long as they need in order to continue pursuing the individual, and their many joints allow them to bend around corners or any other obstacles.

Should the individual manage to fight the arms off or escape, new arms will materialize nearby the victim to aid in the capture.

Once the arms have subdued the targeted person and gotten them back to the area where they appeared they will begin savagely assaulting them, beating and clawing at them until nothing remains of the victim but a bloody pile of flesh and bones.

To date, the Foundation is not aware of any targeted individuals surviving an attack by SCP-517-01 entities.

In the event that the fortune telling machine was activated multiple times on the same day, multiple instances of arms appearing will occur at different locations at the same time, with each group hunting their own individual target.

Efforts have been made to figure out exactly where the arms manifest from, and during testing cameras were set up around the targeted individual in order to try and locate a place of origin.

Unfortunately the arms somehow seemed aware that they were being watched, and the arms always emanated from around a corner or other place that was out of the field of view of the cameras.

Tests on SCP-517 did reveal one piece of evidence though, as fragments of DNA were recovered from the areas where SCP-517-01 instances appeared, DNA that turned out to be human in origin.

The origins of the DNA and the identity of the owner have yet to be determined.

Research and containment of SCP-517 has proven to be quite difficult, as evidenced by an event designated Incident 517-1997-M. As Foundation agent Dr. Meil supervised the transport of SCP-517 to a new containment storage locker, the fortune teller suddenly activated and it was suspected that Dr. Meil had become a target.

Security personnel were alerted and a defensive strategy was devised to protect her from instances of SCP-517-01 that were expected to manifest that night at 1:43 AM.

Dr. Meil was taken to a helicopter on the roof of a Foundation cafeteria and given the protection of multiple security personnel as they waited for the arms to manifest.

Right on cue, the arms appeared in a storage area inside the cafeteria and began stretching their way towards the roof.

Security teams inside the cafeteria opened fire on the arms, which took damage just like normal human arms, though they would quickly be replaced by more.

More instances of SCP-517-01 began appearing, coming out from under parked vehicles and other storage areas, as the number of arms coming out of the original manifestation site continued to increase until there were over a hundred.

The arms did not seem to want to fight back against the security teams though.

They seemed singular in their focus - get to the roof where Dr. Meil was waiting.

As the ever-increasing amount of limbs overwhelmed the security teams and breached the roof, the order was given for the helicopter to take off.

The helicopter rose into the air, but the arms began manifesting from somewhere underneath the helicopter itself.

The arms broke through the windows and pulled Dr. Meil out, passing her down to the waiting arms on the roof that then carried her through the cafeteria's ventilation system.

A security personnel in the cafeteria attempted to sever the limbs with a knife and rescue Dr. Meil, but the arms were no longer ignoring their attackers and grabbed him as well, dragging him down towards the storage locker along with the doctor.

In the end, four members of the security team along with Dr. Meil were pulled into the storage area by the arms.

Their remains were collected the next morning and the Foundation made their best efforts to separate and identify what was left for individual funerary services. SCP-517, which has been classified as safe, is kept in a dedicated containment cell at all times, facing away from the doorway, with an opaque black sheet bound around it.

Following the events of Incident 517-1997-M, all testing has been halted, without the express written permission of the Site Director.

Peering into our future can be a fun activity, even when we know it's all just a bit of make believe.

When you pull your fortune from a booth containing an elderly automaton though, you might just find that this time, Grammie Knows your fate for real.

4. THE PROTOTYPE-SCP-001

The guerrilla soldiers fire their rifles blindly into the jungle.
They don't know what exactly they're shooting at, but something is out there among the trees.
Something they can't see.
Something that's killing them.
One of the young soldiers, barely more than a boy, stops to reload.
As he pulls the magazine from his rifle, a blur passes by.
The soldier next to him suddenly drops to his knees clutching his neck, blood pouring out between his fingers.
A hand grasps the boy's shoulder and he spins around, nearly opening fire on his commander.
The older man tells him they've got to go and the boy joins a small group of soldiers who start running through the jungle, trying to get away from whatever this thing is.
As they run there's another flash of movement and one of the soldiers is pulled into the trees.
He can hear his screams mixed with the otherworldly shrieks but there's nothing they can do, it's already too late for him.
Another soldier disappears into the trees with a blur.
It's just him and the commander now.
They emerge from the jungle into a clearing that contains a small, abandoned farm.
The commander motions for them to head towards the old farm house and the two take cover around the corner of the home.
They crouch with their guns ready, peeking around the corner, looking for any sign of the monster that's killed so many of their comrades.

The boy wants to know what they should do.

He opens his mouth to ask the commander but he puts a finger to his lips and motions for the boy to keep watching.

The boy peeks around the corner of the house but he doesn't see anything emerging from the treeline.

It's quiet, until the commander begins to scream.

The boy turns to see a point forming on his chest.

It's a black circle, no not black, something darker.

It's like it is the absence of any and all light.

The commander screams louder as the point of darkness grows.

The commander's screams fade out even as it looks like he continues to yell.

The boy watches as the commander seems to be collapsing in, sucked into the dark orb in his chest.

The commander's body folds in on itself, growing smaller and smaller until it disappears completely into the black hole, which vanishes along with him.

The boy doesn't know what he just saw but he doesn't have time to think, because emerging from the forest, is the creature.

The boy has never seen anything like it and runs into the farmhouse.

He locks the door and pushes the old kitchen table in front of it, trying to barricade it as best he can.

He looks around and spots a bed against the wall.

It's the best hiding spot he can find so he runs and slides under the bed, pulling

himself as close to the wall as he can.

The boy watches and waits, unsure of what he should do.

It's quiet.

There's no more screaming of soldiers being killed or any more of those guttural, animal-like squeals.

Maybe it decided to go back to wherever it came from.

The boy doesn't dare come out from under the bed though.

As he watches the door, waiting for something to burst through, he sees something else.

Another of those black points appears in the middle of the room.

It looks like it bends the light around it, distorting the room nearby.

The boy watches from under the bed as out of the point, a thin black limb emerges.

First one, then another.

He can see its strange pointed legs with no feet standing just in front of the bed now.

With a high pitched cry, the creature effortlessly tosses the bed aside.

The boy is left exposed, cowering against the wall.

The creature screams, opening its wide mouth that seems to split its eyeless face in two, revealing two rows of jagged teeth.

The boy screams back, crying in fear, and sees that the creature isn't eyeless after all.

Inside its grotesque mouth, a milky-blue ball appears.

There's no iris, but the boy knows whatever this thing is, it's looking at him.

The boy feels his chest grow tight.

He looks down to see that one of the black points is forming on his chest.

He can feel himself being squeezed and crushed, pulled down into this singular point.

All noises, including his screams disappear as he is pulled into this soundless void.

But then he hears something again.

He looks up to see that the creature is being riddled with bullets.

It turns to escape and bursts through the wall of the farmhouse.

The dark orb on the boy vanishes and he sees, standing in the doorway, his friend and savior.

He clutches his bleeding throat with one hand, holding his rifle in the other.

The boy rushes to him as he collapses to the floor.

Blood is pouring out of his neck and he can no longer speak, but he dies knowing he saved his young friend.

The boy starts to feel very tired, and he sits down next to his dead hero.

He's all alone now, his entire group of freedom fighters now wiped out by this demon.

The boy feels nauseous and dizzy.

He coughs into his hand and looks down to see that it's covered in his own blood.

A group of boys run down a jungle path, laughing and playing when they suddenly stop and grow quiet.

There's something up ahead of them.

It's a man, lying on the side of the road.

The boys look scared, unsure if they should check it out, but then the smallest of all of them emerges from the group and bravely marches up to the man.

Not wanting to let the youngest of their friends make them look like cowards, the rest of the boys soon follow.

The man on the side of the road is moaning and looks to be in pain.

As they get closer they can see that he must have been in a terrible accident.

His skin is gray, and it looks like his long thin arms only have three fingers.

What should they do?

The small boy picks up a stick and reaches out with it to poke the man, not wanting to touch him with his own hands, but before he can the man rolls over, opening his mouth with a horrible shriek to reveal the glassy blue eye inside as the boys turn and run, hands over their ears.

Several weeks later, the small Guatemalan town holds a meeting.

The crowd of people in the room are angrily yelling at the mayor who stands at a podium, demanding answers from him about what happened to their dead or missing loved ones.

A series of photos are hung on the wall behind the mayor in remembrance of those who have disappeared into the forest, or mysteriously died from a rapid illness, including the brave young boy.

One man shouts at the mayor, wanting to know where his daughter was, another asks how her healthy husband could drop dead from an illness after being perfectly healthy only days before.

The mayor tries to calm the frustrated townspeople, telling them that he knows there have been rumors of a demon out in the forest, but that's all they are… rumors.

The mayor warns them though that something is out there, though he doesn't know what.

There is an animal or man that is making people sick.

It may also be hunting people, neither he nor the police know exactly what is going on.

But there is good news, a group of men have come to help them.

The mayor points towards a stern looking man in a military uniform who is standing with a small group of other soldiers and a scientist off to the side of the stage.

The mayor explains that this man, General Machoi, is from America, and that he's going to help them.

The crowd doesn't cheer in the way that the mayor seems to have expected, but they at least stop their yelling as the General steps to the podium and thanks the mayor for the introduction.

The general looks over the crowd who are waiting and hungry for answers about the monster that's suddenly begun plaguing their town.

He tells them that it is true that he's been sent here by the US Government in order to investigate what's been happening, and stop whatever threat is out there in the jungle by any means necessary.

He can't promise that he'll be able to bring back any of their missing loved ones, but he can at least prevent whatever this is from taking any more.

He then gestures to the rest of his group and tells the crowd that the men he has brought with him have been specially trained to deal with this exact type of situation, and that they don't need to worry any longer.

The only thing everyone needs to do is stay out of their way, and all will be taken care of.

With that, he walks off the stage as the crowd erupts into more shouting.

General Machoi stops at the scientists waiting next to the stage.

"Well Dr. Keter, what do you think?"

The scientist adjusts his glasses and answers "This is what we've been preparing for.

The Overseers kept telling us this day would come.

It looks like it finally has."

The group of soldiers led by General Machoi make their way through the dense forest.

Dr. Keter is just ahead of them, using a Geiger counter to follow the creature, the audible clicks of the radioactive entity telling him which way it came.

They track the source of the radiation to a clearing in the jungle where a small village once stood.

Most of the buildings are overgrown with plants and thick vines, but with it growing dark, this seems as safe a place as they will find to make camp for the night.

The soldiers fan out to search what's left of the town as Dr. Keter continues looking around for where the radioactive trail might lead them next.

As General Machoi is checking out one of the many dark, old buildings, one of the other soldiers cries out.

"Hey General!

It looks like this generator still works!"

With the sound of an old diesel motor coming to life, lights in the village suddenly flicker on.

They now have fortifications and light.

Though he'd never admit it, General Machoi was feeling nervous about spending the night in the jungle, but now at least some of those nerves were being washed away by the old, flickering yellow lights.

Later that night, the General is questioning Dr. Keter on where the creature went.

Dr. Keter is confused though.

His readings showed high traces of radiation leading into this village.

The creature came here, he was sure of it, but now he can't figure out where it went.

It's as if it came into the village and then simply vanished.

Outside, one of the soldiers on watch tells the rest of the group who are sitting around a fire to shut up, that he thinks he saw something in the woods.

Everyone immediately springs into action, taking defensive positions and aiming their rifles into the dark treeline.

"There it is again" he says, as a flash of darkness moves just beyond the clearing.

"No, it's over here" says another soldier on the opposite side.

How could the creature be moving so fast around them?

Are there multiple of whatever this is out there?

The soldiers form a circle to make sure that the thing can't get behind them.

What they can't see, is the point of darkness forming behind all of their backs, and the thin, pointed legs stepping out of it.

The general's radio comes to life.

"I think we've got something out here Gen - " but his message is cut off by screams and the sound of gunfire.

General Machoi tells Dr. Keter to stay inside and runs out of the building, where he finally gets a glimpse of the "demon" that they've been tracking.

The tall, thin creature is massacring his squad.

It dashes between them at an inhuman speed, using its three fingered hands to rip the limbs off of some soldiers and slash at others with its razor sharp claws, opening up their necks or disemboweling them before moving on to the next.

The General fires his rifle at the creature and misses, but it's enough to get it to

retreat.

General Machoi runs back inside the building where Dr. Keter is waiting.

"What was it, what did you see out there?"

The General doesn't know how to begin describing the monster that just killed all of his men.

It's like nothing he has ever seen before and something that no amount of training could prepare him for.

As the two men ponder what to do next, the Geiger counter on the table suddenly starts to click, softly at first, but then more and more, as if a huge amount of radiation has suddenly flooded the room.

The General grabs the Doctor and drags him out, leaping out of the building just before it collapses in on itself, disappearing into the micro-singularity that formed inside.

The two men look up to see it standing right in front of them, its huge mouth open to reveal its glassy blue eye.

"Look out!"

Dr. Keter cries, but he isn't talking about the demon as he and the General roll to the side, just avoiding the power line that has been cut loose by the destroyed building.

The power line hits the ground and immediately begins to spark, sending out bright pulses of white, electrical light.

The creature cries out with a gut wrenching scream and collapses to the ground, huddling up into a ball as it tries to cover up its mouth with its thin arms.

"Is it the electricity?" the General asks, confused about what suddenly stopped the killer's rampage, but Dr. Keter realizes it isn't the sparking power line that the creature has been immobilized by, it's the flashing lights.

The General doesn't wait for his answer though, and fires the weighted net from his gun, trapping the howling creature.

Dr. Keter examines the creature at the field research center that has been set up several miles from the village.

A strobe light has been affixed to the inside of the creature's cage, but even when the doctor turns the light off, the grayish brown skinned entity still remains curled up in a ball on the floor.

The doctor wonders if perhaps the creature is hungry, but it shows no interest in any of the various meats, fruits, and vegetables they've presented to it.

The doctor stands in the doorway of the tent that has been up to house the creature's cage and gives an update to General Machoi, who is anxious to get the creature moved to the United States and a more secure containment environment.

Dr. Keter stresses that he fears the journey might kill this creature though, and put an end to the incredible research and testing they can perform on this amazing living specimen.

The General turns to leave but stops to salute the body of one of his soldiers being carried by on a stretcher.

Dr. Keter himself turns to go back to his research when he notices something.

The creature's mouth is ever so slightly open.

Dr. Keter has yet another idea.

That night, Dr. Keter enters the temporary morgue and takes a severed arm from one of the dead soldiers.

Back in the research tent, he presents the arm to the creature, sliding it through the cage bars.

The creature doesn't react, but Dr. Keter continues to watch and wait.

After a time, the creature finally stirs.

It's the first time he has seen it move since it was captured.

The creature reaches out with its long, three fingered hand and grabs the arm before starting to feed on it.

"You like that, don't you?"

Dr. Keter asks, and bizarrely, the creature seems to respond, giving an almost baby-like coo.

"There's lots more of that if you behave.

All I want to do is study you, learn how you work."

The creature continues to feed, starting to crunch on the bones now that all of the meat is gone.

"Yes, I believe you'll be good" the doctor says as he approaches the cage.

"You're going to make me world famous.

Soon everyone will know the name Hermann Ket -"

The creature's hand shoots out from between the bars so quickly he never even saw it.

Dr. Keter starts to scream as it grasps and claws at him.

A soldier standing guard outside runs in but a black point of light immediately appears on his torso, causing him to fold in on himself into the singularity.

The creature drops the bloodied Dr. Keter to the floor, who reaches for the emergency strobe light activation button as another singularity opens up inside of the cage.

The creature appears to willfully step into it before emerging out of another just outside of the bars.

More soldiers rush into the tent in time to see the creature feeding on the still living Dr. Keter.

One presses the button to activate the high powered strobe lights which cause the creature to start screaming and thrashing about, trying to escape the flashing lights.

Multiple nets are fired onto the creature, pinning it to the ground as its screams slowly fade back to whimpers.

On Overseer orders, the creature is moved to ADRX-19, a secure base located somewhere in North America.

The site's director gives a presentation to a group and explains that thanks to the work of the late Dr. Keter, they now know that the creature exhibits signs of fear and sickness when in the presence of strobing lights, and that it is unable to produce the microsingularities that it uses for defense and teleportation when it is in this sickened state.

When healthy though, the creature is extremely dangerous thanks to its superhuman speed, strength, and cunning.

It was also discovered that it is unable to teleport through lead, which its new containment cell has been lined with, and extreme security procedures have been implemented including the installation of a reinforced steel blast door and constant patrols of the outside of the cell by armed guards who are equipped with high-powered strobe lights.

The site director leaves the room and the Overseers discuss the fate of the creature

which has been given the designation number 86243AR-001, though most have taken to calling it simply 001.

One of the Overseers argues that the creature must be secured and contained in order to protect humanity.

Who knows how many more of these might be out there.

They now know that the rumors of these types of entities aren't merely isolated events, and there could be countless more of these anomalies.

Hundreds, maybe even thousands.

The rest of the Overseers unanimously agree.

One of them picks up the report that was left behind by the site director.

"Redact this report immediately and start a new document archive. This is only The Prototype.

I have the feeling there will likely be many more of these…"

5. KILLER CENTIPEDE SCP-4310 THE HERO'S JOURNEY

The 13 year old boy gets a running start, before leaping across from one moss covered boulder to another.
He barely makes the jump and turns around to admire how far he leaped.
He continues along through the woods, hopping over streams and making sure to swing on any hanging vines he can find, whether he needs to or not.
He picks up a branch and starts to swing it against a tree, engaging in a life and death duel with the evil knight of the woods.
After slaying the knight, the boy solemnly salutes his fallen foe before mounting his trusty steed to ride deeper into the forest.
He's all alone out here, and must be thousands of miles from civilization.
The valiant knight unmounts from his horse and walks towards the culmination of his quest.
The Tree of Lost Memories.
Legend tells that anything buried beneath this tree will cease to exist.
All memories of anything associated with the object buried will disappear from the minds of anyone involved and no one will ever bring them up again or wonder where the memories went.
The knight takes a letter sealed with wax from where he was keeping it safely inside of his armor and kneels in front of the tree.
He brushes the leaves and dirt away from a spot near the base of the tree and digs a
small hole with his hands before placing the letter inside the hole.
The boy looks down at the letter, satisfied with his work.
He starts covering the letter inside the hole with dirt when he suddenly stands up.
Was that a noise?
He listens again, it's not just a noise, it's a voice.
The knight unsheathes his sword and starts making his way in the direction he can hear the sounds coming from.

He follows a game trail through the woods towards the noise.

There's no doubt, it's definitely a voice, and he can make it out clearly now.

"The Wheel of history turns, and ages come and pass, leaving memories that become legend" The knight rounds a corner and the woods open up into a clearing.

In the middle of the grassy open area is a stone archway unconnected to any walls.

When looking through the archway though, one doesn't simply see the other side of the clearing.

No, inside the archway is a beautiful, white alabaster castle perched on rock overlooking the sea, its red roofed turrets jutting high up into the clouds.

And standing next to the archway that seems to lead to another land, is an old man dressed in a long flowing robe, a wizard's robe.

The boy steps out of the woods into the clearing.

What is this old man doing out here?

And what's going on with this archway?

It really does look like it is showing something it shouldn't be able to.

"Legends fade to myth, and even myth is long forgotten when the Age that gave it birth comes again."

"Are you talking to me?" the boy asks.

"Venture forth and face your true calling," the wizard responds.

"You are the one that has been prophesied, but have you what it takes to enter this land of adventure?"

The boy looks around, there's no one else here, this old man must be speaking to him, right?

The boy tosses his stick to the ground and steps closer to the old man and the archway.

He can see now that the surface of the archway appears to be shimmering, as if it were a vertical surface of water.

"Only the truest of hearts may enter the magical archway, but for the fair and brave, a great quest awaits."

"A quest? For me?" the boy asks, but again the old man doesn't respond.

He doesn't seem to be looking at him either, is this wise old man in the woods blind?

The boy gets much closer now, close enough to wave his hand in front of the old man's face, but there's no reaction, he really must be blind.

The boy looks back at the portal in the archway.

He can see the waves breaking on the rocks and birds flying in the sky.

He can even make out, up in one of the highest windows on the tallest tower, what looks to be a... a girl.

She's waving her ribbon in the air.

She's beckoning him, she needs the brave knight to come save her.

"Pursue your destiny, and become the hero you were always meant to be!"

The boy is entranced by the beauty of this land, the castle, the clouds drifting between the white towers, the perfectly blue sea, the beautiful princess locked in her tower, waiting for him.

The boy reaches his hand through the surface of the archway and it passes through as if nothing were there, but on the other side it turns into the gauntleted hand of a knight.

He pulls his hand back out and it looks like his own hand once again.

The boy thinks about his mother, yelling at him for drawing pictures of the lands he wished he could live in when he should be studying, he thinks of his teacher grabbing the fantasy book out of his hand and dropping it in the trash calling it a waste of time, he thinks of his friends laughing when he came to school dressed as a knight.

He knew he was destined for something greater, and here it finally is.

He really is a knight.

He's the hero that was prophesied.

He will become a legend.

He's special.

The knight girds himself and steps forward into the archway.

As he does he hears the old man still talking.

"The Wheel of history turns, and ages come and pass, leaving memories that —"

The boy passes through the archway and the castle, the sea, the princess... all of them disappear in an instant.

The boy spins around but the archway constricts, snapping shut in a tight ball with him still inside.

The old man sinks into the ground as the archway seems to rotate.

The archway then also disappears into the earth, as something else emerges.

A giant centipede appears out of the ground, its scaly body the color of stone with movable plates on its posterior end that resembles the movement of cloth.

The centipede opens its mouth and there's a sound like the cry of a child before it dives down and disappears under the dirt.

Have you ever thought that you were destined for something more?

Do you feel as if the worlds described in fantasy books and that are brought to life in movies and in video games are somehow the places you actually belong?

You're far from alone, but be careful, because it's exactly those thoughts that make you the prime target for SCP-4310, a deadly predator that preys on those with the desire to embark on a Hero's Journey.

SCP-4310 is an anomalous creature that resembles a common centipede in many ways, though it has a number of traits that distinguish it from the kind you might find under a rock in the forest.

Perhaps most obvious is its size.

06:30While some centipedes can grow as long as a foot, SCP-4310 is over 20 feet in length.

This massive, carnivorous centipede, which is native to Great Britain and Ireland, also has a hunting method that is quite distinct from any arthropod, insect, or known animal at all for that matter.

SCP-4310 hunts by cocooning itself in a pair of keratin flaps that cover its entire body except for its tail end, which is left exposed.

The centipede then buries itself in the ground keeping its head and the majority of its body under the ground, except for a portion that arcs above the ground in a semi-circle shape as well as its exposed posterior.

The centipede's end resembles an old man wearing robes, and the centipede is able to manipulate its rear legs in a way that resembles the movement of a mouth and jaw, giving the impression that the old man is speaking.

The rest of its body is contorted and the legs are arranged in such a way to resemble a stone archway standing unsupported on the ground next to the old man.

Through a process that is yet to be understood by the Foundation, the centipede is able to produce a spatial anomaly in the area where its body is taking on the form of an archway.

This spatial anomaly is actually a portal of sorts, a portal that leads directly into SCP-4310's stomach.

As soon as its prey enters the spatial anomaly, the centipede closes the portal.

Inside, paralysis inducing enzymes incapacitate the prey as powerful stomach acids break down its meal over the course of several days.

You may be thinking, "I would never walk into an archway next to an old man in the middle of the forest" but SCP-4310 has two powerful mechanisms perfectly suited to luring its prey.

First, it is capable of emitting a pheromone that induces a state of mild euphoria while at the same time suppressing fear and encouraging curiosity.

This appears to affect all warm blooded mammals, but humans and their natural inclination towards exploration makes them especially vulnerable to the effects.

The second method 4310 utilizes to acquire food is producing a very unique set of sounds.

These sounds, which are made by rubbing together portions inside of its tail segment, resemble English speech, and are almost always phrases that describe quests, prophecies, and heroic deeds that can only be undertaken by journeying into the archway.

SCP-4310 calls can last for as long as three minutes before they begin to repeat the series of heroic phrases.

And each instance of SCP-4310 appears to have its own unique set of calls to embark on adventure, but with all encouraging entrance into the archway.

It is unknown just how SCP-4310 learns these phrases, since other than this advanced hunting technique, no instance of the anomalous creature has shown intelligence levels above that of an ordinary centipede.

Interestingly, the same heroic speech sounds appear to also act as SCP-4310's mating call, and it is unknown if the luring of would-be adventurers by the noises is merely a lucky by-product, or if it specifically uses the sounds for both mating and eating.

SCP-4310 became known to the SCP Foundation in the 1950s following an investigation into multiple missing persons in Belfast, Northern Ireland.

Agents searched a nearby forest and soon discovered human teeth in animal droppings concentrated around a wooded grotto.

The grotto was excavated and three instances of SCP-4310 were found hibernating beneath the ground.

It's since been learned that after eating their fill, SCP-4310 will enter a hibernation state that can last as long as ten years, and it appeared that these three instances ate well, since the remains of over seventy children were eventually found in the immediate area.

SCP-4310 has been classified as Euclid, and currently, one instance is kept in a containment cell for observation and testing.

The cell has been filled with a thick layer of soil resembling that found in the temperate forests of Great Britain and once per week, five piglets are introduced into the centipede's enclosure.

Mobile Task Force Labda-12, codenamed "Pest Control," is dispatched to areas where there are reports of old men resembling wizards encouraging people to step through a magical archway, and the MTF agents are to exterminate any instances that they find in the wild.

The Foundation's Department of Analytics also monitors all contemporary British children's and young adult literature, especially the fantasy genre, for references to portals in the woods that lead to wondrous locations, and Lambda-12 is alerted to any that may be inspired by or referencing real SCP-4310 instances.

All of us fantasize from time to time about embarking on an epic quest that will allow us to escape our regular lives.

While it is fun to dream about being swept off to another world, be very careful if you meet an old man in the woods who tells you that your quest begins with stepping through a magical archway, or you might just find that your hero's journey starts and ends in the belly of a giant centipede.

6. THE BODY HARVESTER SCP-5172

A businessman steps out of his hotel room holding a silver ice bucket.

He looks up and down the empty hallway until he spots what he was searching for - an ice machine.

He slips his room key into his pocket and heads down the hall towards the machine.

As he waits for the machine to fill his bucket with ice, he glances around and spots something.

There at the end of the hall it looks like someone is sticking their head out from around the corner, watching him.

But then they suddenly disappear.

He doesn't think much of it, it's probably just some kid playing around.

His ice bucket is only a quarter full, these old machines can be really slow.

He looks around again and sees the same head poking around the corner, looking at him.

He thinks it might be a young girl, but as he squints to get a better look, she disappears around the corner once again.

The ice machine finally finishes filling his bucket.

He picks it up and starts to walk back towards his room but stops.

He turns around and looks down the hall to see the same girl there again, watching him, with a creepy, unblinking stare.

"Do you want something?" the man asks down the hallway, but there's no response from the girl.

She simply keeps looking at him.

"Are you just going to keep staring at me?"

That's exactly what she does.

The businessman is really starting to get annoyed now.

All he wanted to do was unwind with a drink after a long day at a job site.

Why does this girl want to keep messing with him?

He starts walking down the hall towards her.

"I don't know what you think you're playing at," the businessman says as he walks down the hallway in her direction.

When gets halfway to her she disappears behind the corner once again, but the businessman keeps walking and talking to her.

"But if you don't stop messing with me I'll - " he rounds the corner and sees... nothing.

There's a short hallway that leads to a maintenance closet, but no girl.

Did she somehow slip inside the closet?

He didn't hear the door, but she couldn't be anywhere else.

He sets down the ice bucket on the floor and reaches towards the handle with more than a little apprehension.

He feels uneasy for some reason, and maybe even a little scared.

But there's nothing to be afraid of, it was just a girl, wasn't it?

He grabs the handle and opens the door.

"Aha I've got... you..."

There's nothing in the closet, just a couple of mops, a bucket, and some cleaning supplies.

He pushes the mops aside, as if she could somehow be hiding behind them, but no, there's no place to hide or secret doors to be found.

He really must have imagined the whole thing.

It was a long day.

And a long flight before that.

He needed that drink.

He sticks his roomkey into the door and pulls it out.

A green light flashes and the lock clicks open.

He grabs the handle to open the door when he realizes he's forgotten something.

The ice bucket, the whole reason he left his room to begin with.

He walks back down the hallway and past the ice ma - wait a second.

Where's the ice machine?

Isn't this where it was?

The alcove where he could have sworn he got ice just minutes before is empty.

He looks around, up and down the hallway.

Did he somehow get turned around?

He walks to the end of the hall and turns the corner.

Sitting there on the floor in front of the maintenance closet door, is the ice bucket.

He looks around, confusion on his face, and picks up the ice bucket.

Back at his room he puts his roomkey into the door.

The lock flashes red.

He tries the key again, and once more it flashes red.

He tries the key a third time and as he does so, the door opens.

He looks up to see a large man standing in front of him.

"Do you need something?"

The businessman is confused, "what are you doing in my room?" he asks.

"Your room?" the large man responds.

"Yeah, room 237."

The large man looks annoyed.

He shoves past the businessman and points across the hall.

The businessman follows his finger's direction to see that he's pointing at another door, one that has the number "237" next to it on the wall.

The businessman looks at the number next to the door he's been trying to unlock.

-239.

The businessman laughs nervously at his mistake as the large man pushes past him again and closes the door behind him.

Back in his room, the businessman can finally sit down and pour himself a drink.

He takes two ice cubes from the bucket and drops them in his glass before taking a long sip.

Ahhh.

He turns on the TV, but after watching for a few minutes he finds that he's having a hard time concentrating.

Whatever this show is, it moves too fast and he can't keep track of what's happening.

He turns off the TV and picks up a book instead, maybe some reading will help him to relax and get his bearings.

He still feels really... off.

He opens the book, but gets confused.

Is this the same book he bought in the airport?

It looks like it's written in a foreign language.

It's just a bunch of squiggles.

He tosses the book on the table and yawns.

It's not that late, but he's feeling really tired.

He gets up, kicks off his shoes, and lies down on the bed without bothering to undress.

He's too tired for that.

He mumbles to himself for a moment, half awake, talking about how he needs to return that foreign book when he goes back to the airport.

What were they trying to do selling him something he can't even read?

He continues to mumble about the things he'll do to the cashier who sold him the book for a while until he finally drifts off to sleep.

His eyes open.

It's dark.

He must have been sleeping for a while.

The room is cold too.

He goes to pull the blankets up over him but immediately realizes that he can't move.

Try as he might, his body won't respond.

Not a single muscle.

Only his eyes seem to work.

He's completely paralyzed, he can't even yell for help.

What happened?

And what is he going to do?

Did he have a stroke?

Is he dying?

As his mind races through all the different possibilities he suddenly sees something.

From his bed in the dark room, he can just barely make out the door to his hotel room, and he is terrified by what he can see coming through it.

A figure has appeared in the door.

Literally in the door, as if it is phasing through the solid wood.

The man is scared to death as the thing fully enters his room and turns to look right at him.

The man wants to scream but his mouth is still completely numb.

The figure starts crawling towards him.

He can see now that it's small, smooth, and completely white.

He fights as hard as he can, willing his body to move, but nothing happens.

He can't so much as whisper.

The thing climbs up onto the bed and sits down right on his chest.

He prays that he is dreaming, telling himself to wake up over and over again as the creature leans its face in close to his.

It seems as if it is somehow looking at him with its smooth, eyeless sockets.

It tilts its head slightly to the side and -

Welcome!

I'm Dr. Max, and we couldn't be happier that you've decided to stay with us as we delve into SCP-5172, an extremely dangerous anomaly that is known by the extremely non-threatening name of...
North American Hotel Ice Machines.

SCP-5172 is a phenomenon that only affects guests staying at hotels located on the North American continent.

It is unknown how or what causes these guests to become affected, but those that are will begin to notice something - ice machines in the hallway of the hotel they are staying in.

Now you might think this sounds perfectly normal, after all, don't most hotels have ice machines?

If you just had this thought then I have bad news for you, because there is a high probability that you too may have been affected by SCP-5172.

You see, ice machines are actually extremely uncommon in hotels and it is likely that you have never actually seen one, or at least, not a real one.

Allow me to explain.

In the 1950s, the founder of the Holiday Inn chain of hotels, Kennon Williams, had an idea that he thought would set his hotel apart and attract customers which was to offer more perks and amenities than his competitors.

For example, he implemented a new policy where children would be allowed to stay for free, something most hotels charged extra for.

Hotels at the time also had a policy of making their guests pay for ice, but Williams decided to change that... by installing ice machines in his hotels.

Sadly, the marketing stunt didn't work.

The cost of the machines wasn't made up for in new customers and the plan was discontinued by the mid 1960s.

The vast majority of the machines were removed, with the rest being pulled from the hotels as they would break down, since they were no longer worth the expense of maintaining.

Despite the fact that they only existed in hotels for a brief period of time, there is still a widely held belief among the public that ice machines can be found in nearly every hotel.

In a poll of the general population conducted by the Foundation, over 80% of adults claimed to have memories of seeing an ice machine in a hotel, a number that is quite literally, impossible.

Just where this mass delusion came from or why it persists is currently unknown, but it's theorized to be related to the SCP-5172 phenomenon in some way.

The SCP Foundation first became aware of SCP-5172 in 1973 after a series of unsolved murders occurred at hotels in Winnipeg, Manitoba, Canada.

Foundation investigators soon discovered the prevalence of false ice machine memories and installed a number of hidden cameras around the hotels in both their public spaces as well as in the room themselves.

It was after viewing the footage captured by these cameras that the Foundation finally got their first look at just what happens during an occurrence of SCP-5172, which has been dubbed a Zalmunna Event.

The Zalmunna Event is triggered whenever a guest at the hotel sees and then uses an ice machine.

The moment they use the ice machine, the event can not be stopped unless certain actions are taken, but more on that later.

The targeted individual who used the ice machine will immediately begin to have the sense that they are being watched.

This usually comes in the form of an unknown individual who appears to be looking at them from the end of the hall where the ice machine is located.

Third party observers are unable to see the person who is supposedly watching the target, nor do they appear on any recording devices, visual or otherwise.

The targets have described the watchers in various ways, leading the Foundation to believe that they may actually be nothing more than hallucinations.

Shortly after, the targeted individual will begin to experience feelings of confusion

and fatigue not dissimilar to the symptoms of early-stage dementia.

The longer it takes the target to return to their hotel room, the more pronounced these feelings will become, and they will soon have issues completing everyday tasks and will experience short term memory loss.

Despite these feelings of fatigue and disorientation, targets report that their mind feels too active to fall asleep, anywhere other than a hotel room bed, that is.

This feeling will usually cause the target to seek out their own hotel room, though they may have difficulty finding it due to their confused state.

They don't need to sleep in their own room for the next stage of the Zalmunna Event to be triggered through, sleeping in any hotel room will do.

Once the target lies down in a hotel room bed, they will immediately enter the hypnagogic state, which is the confusing and dreamlike state that one experiences in between full sleep and waking.

The temperature of the room will begin to lower during this period as well until it reaches approximately 11 degrees celsius or 51.8 degrees fahrenheit.

After about an hour, the target will enter into a state of deep sleep, at which point SCP-5172-1 will finally make its appearance.

The humanoid-like entity is quite diminutive in size, standing just four feet tall and appearing to weigh a little over 60 pounds.

Its arms are twice as long as normal humans though, and the top of its head is enlarged as well.

Though it is not visible to observers present in the room, cameras are able to record the creature.

After phasing through the door of the hotel room, the 5172-1 entity will begin crawling towards the sleeping person who will wake up to find that they are in a state of sleep paralysis.

The entity will climb up onto the bed and sit on the person's chest.

It will move its smooth skinned face close to the target's before opening its mouth, revealing a long, thin proboscis-like appendage that it inserts into the target's eye socket.

It's long been theorized that it may be administering some type of paralytic or anesthesia directly into the brain so that it can then engage in the next stage of the Zalmunna Event... harvesting.

The 5172-1 entity's chest then opens to reveal a pair of tools.

It will take the tools out of its chest and use them to begin extracting four centimeter cubes directly from the target's body.

Flesh, muscle, organs, and even bone will all be cut and scooped out with the same ease, which it then places inside of its own chest cavity.

While it starts the process extremely slow, collecting just two cubes per minute at first, it quickly ups its pace to as many as fifty cubes per minute, leading to the entire harvesting process typically lasting two to three hours.

Once it has finished harvesting, the creature will simply place its tools back inside its chest cavity, crawl back towards the hotel room door, and phase through it once more.

But the horror is far from over.

SCP-5172-1 collects all of the organic material from the target during the harvesting process, all except for the central nervous system which includes the spinal cord, peripheral nerves, the retinas, and the brain.

These are left lying on the hotel room bed after 5172-1 carefully cut and scooped around them.

And the truly horrifying aspect of the Zalmunna Event, is that the target is still alive at this point, and will continue to live for several more hours in this condition.

Even worse, reports from targets who had the Zalmunna Event interrupted while in the middle of the harvesting process described being fully conscious the entire time.

It now appears that the proboscis-like appendage that 5172-1 inserts into the target's eye does not appear to be an anesthetic agent at all, since the same rescued targets reported feeling excruciating pain.

Instead, it seems that the purpose of the entity's appendage is to ensure that the victim stays conscious through the whole process, fully aware of each cube being removed from their body, helpless to do a thing to stop it.

As mentioned, the triggering of a Zalmunna Event is not a guaranteed death sentence, and can be stopped.

While much faster than humans, SCP-5172-1 entities aren't especially strong and sustain damage much like a human would.

Once it begins harvesting, the entity will become visible to others and can be terminated by the same methods that would kill a human, such as with gunshots or stab wounds.

However simply killing the entity isn't enough.

The affected ice machine must be physically removed from the premises in order to prevent a new instance of SCP-5172-1 from materializing.

Once triggered through the use of an affected ice machine, the only way to completely stop a Zalmunna Event is for the target to leave the hotel and sleep in a private residence, which will prevent SCP-5172-1 from appearing.

If the target sleeps in any bed in the same, or even a different hotel, the event will continue.

Efforts are underway to better understand SCP-5172-1 entities by capturing a live specimen, but so far all attempts have resulted in failure.

Captured entities are capable of manifesting their tools and cutting out of containment, while all attempts at binding or otherwise tying down the creatures has led to them dying within several minutes.

Autopsies of dead instances have revealed that like us, they have a circulatory system, though its heart is located in its head, which explains how they can be killed by being shot or stabbed, but they lack respiratory and digestive organs.

As you can imagine, the existence of SCP-5172 presents a problem for Foundation personnel and their business travel.

Agents who must stay in hotels rather than SCP safehouses are briefed on the anomaly and required to wear heart rate monitors that can detect when an elevated heart rate occurs that may be connected to a Zalmunna Event.

Social media, text messages, and other forms of communication from devices that are connected to hotel wifi systems are monitored at all times for any references to "ice machines" and any mention triggers the dispatching of a containment team to the site who will attempt to identify and remove both the ice machine and the targeted individual from the premises.

All ice machines discovered at locations thought to be affected by SCP-5172 are then relocated to Site-30.

One final note, while SCP-5172 has long been thought to be a North American exclusive phenomenon, there has recently been one confirmed instance of an affected ice machine in Amsterdam, the Netherlands.

Making it even stranger is the fact that the Dutch do not seem to have the same mass public perception of the prevalence of hotel ice machines that North Americans do, and it is still unclear if this was a single, isolated event, or a sign that the Keter Class anomaly is spreading to other locations.

Only time will tell, but in the meantime, even if you're staying outside of North America and want a frosty drink, consider paying the outrageous fees and grabbing an already cold one from the minibar.

If you don't, you might find that you're paying for your refreshing beverage with much more than a pound of flesh.

7. SUNKEN CHILDREN'S PERIMETER
SCP-1451

Two recreational divers are swimming along the seafloor nearly a hundred feet below the surface.

This husband and wife duo are no strangers to scuba diving, and they move effortlessly through the water as they marvel at the various fish and plant life that normally remain unseen by humans.

The woman taps her husband on the shoulder and points in the direction of a forest of kelp before starting to swim towards it.

The man is about to follow when he sees something out of the corner of his eye.

He stops and turns to get a better look.

A few dozen meters away, is a group of people.

The man is confused.

He looks back towards his wife who is motioning for him to follow her.

He raises a single finger as if to say "I'll be with you in a minute" and starts to swim in the direction of the strange crowd of people standing on the seafloor.

He still can't make out exactly what he's looking at.

A light current is causing silt to kick up and hang in the water, obscuring his view.

As he gets closer though, everything becomes clear.

It really is a group of people, standing perfectly still, 30 meters underwater.

But they aren't living people of course, they are statues.

The man can see now that these are statues of children.

They are standing in a circle, facing outwards, and each one is holding hands with the statues next to them, forming an unbroken ring.

He swims closer to get a better look.

The statues are covered in algae and other plant life.

He doesn't know who or why someone would make this strange art piece, but whatever their reasons, it looks like it's been down here a long time.

He swims around the circle and counts more than twenty in total, with each one looking to be unique.

While the center of the circle of statues is empty, there's pieces of bricks and concrete scattered all around it.

Did there used to be something down here?

A building or some kind of structure that once housed the statues and has now collapsed?

It seems impossible that anything could have ever been built down here.

He looks back in the direction of his wife but he can't see her.

She must be somewhere among the kelp investigating her own mysteries.

He's about to head in her direction when he notices something.

The inside of the circle isn't empty.

Something is inside, sticking out of the sand.

He swims up above the ring to get a better look.

There's definitely something buried in the circle of statues, he can see now that it is the corner of what looks to be a metal box.

He swims down closer to the box and reaches a hand out towards it, when he suddenly stops, and looks up.

The woman swims out of the dense kelp forest carrying a brightly colored shell.

She can't wait to show her husband how beautiful it is.

She looks around but there's no sign of him.

She looks in the direction that he swam and spots the same strange group of people that he did.

As she swims towards them she also quickly realizes that these are just statues, very odd ones, but statues nonetheless.

She also notices the rubble that surrounds them.

The broken chunks of concrete, bricks, some bones… wait, bones?

That's when she spots something else lying on the ocean floor just outside the ring of statues.

It's her husband's scuba tank with his shattered mask resting on top.

Hi!

I'm Dr. Max.

And this is SCP-1451, also known as…

Sunken Children's Perimeter.

SCP-1451 is the designation that has been given to an anomalous set of metal statues that possess very strange and deadly properties.

The twenty-six statues, each of which is unique and have been given the designations SCP-1451-1 through 26, all resemble human children and range in height from 1.32 to 1.43 meters.

They are located within an ocean inlet on the seafloor, and are arranged in a circle

facing outwards, with each holding hands with the ones next to it, forming an unbroken ring.

These statues are anything but stationary though, at least some of the time, and in fact they have three distinct states of motion which the SCP Foundation refers to as Class 1 through 3 scenarios.

The first, a Class 1 scenario, is the designation given when no movement is detected at all.

This is the state that the statues appear to spend the majority of their time in.

The designation will change to Class 2 when some slight movement of the statues is detected.

In this state, they can be seen to slowly raise and lower their hands, while also subtly moving together in a counter-clockwise direction.

Bubbles have been observed coming from the statues mouths during this scenario.

SCP-1451 will be seen to behave this way when a large object comes near it, and it will often mean that the statues are preparing to transition into a Class 3 scenario.

A Class 3 scenario will be triggered when a solid object that weighs more than 40 grams enters the center of the circle.

When the object, whether it be a living one or not, enters this activation area, the statues will fully animate and turn their attention on the object with only one purpose, to destroy it.

When the statues enter a Class 3 scenario, they exhibit incredible strength and agility.

They appear to possess at least a rudimentary form of intelligence as well, as they have been seen utilizing teamwork and advanced tactics.

Once the statues have been activated, they are relentless in the pursuit of their targets, stopping at nothing to neutralize them.

Should you manage to make it out of the activation area, the statues will still continue to give chase, and in one case they followed a target over a kilometer before finally overtaking it.

Once they get their hands on a target, death and destruction are all but assured.

They will rip and tear anything that enters their circle apart, be it man or machine,

with their metallic hands.

Once they have eliminated the object, the statues will then return to their Class 1

scenario position.

Attempts to intercept the statues as they return to their activation area will lead to what the Foundation has dubbed a Class 3.5 scenario, during which they will destroy anyone or anything that tries to intervene or prevent them from reaching their destination.

While SCP-1451 might seem to be one of the simpler anomalies in the SCP Foundation database, there may just be more to this story than first meets the eye, and in fact, the Sunken Children's Perimeter may not even be the first anomaly that was contained here.

Those with Foundation Overseer level clearance have access to some rather interesting documents that help to fill in just what SCP-1451 might really be, and more importantly, what they're protecting.

The documents include a manifest of the materials that were initially recovered from the area where SCP-1451 was discovered.

These materials included roughly 20 kilograms of bricks, 4,000 kilograms of containment-grade concrete, the type normally used in SCP Foundation sites, and most interesting of all, a damaged Scranton box.

For those unaware, Scranton boxes were the precursors to Dr. Scranton's much better known Reality Anchors.

These powerful devices are used to contain reality warping anomalies and prevent them from bending the fabric of our universe to their whims.

Dr. Scranton's initial research into the technology produced an early version that

was used in the containment of anomalies, though we now know that the technology was flawed and could lead to failures in containment.

In the case of SCP-1451, a document was partially recovered from the Scranton box that alludes to just such a failure.

In this instance, a powerful Euclid class reality warper was being held at Area-56,

a location that the Foundation has no record of ever having existed.

The corrupted file seems to suggest that the reality warping SCP's primary anomalous attribute was that things it believed to be real, would become real.

If it misconceived reality in any way, its anomalous abilities would force that misconception to become actual reality.

For example, after the anomalous entity referred to an agent assigned to its containment as a "child," the agent was at risk of undergoing various physical and mental changes to truly become a child.

It appears that the anomaly may have begun conflating various aspects of its containment, mixing up the concepts of containment itself.

The metal of its cage, the concrete of its cell, the "child" agent involved with its containment, the SCP Foundation itself - they all became entangled within its reality warping anomaly's mind, and appear to have been jumbled together in such a way that led to the creation of SCP-1451, a group of metal children who are eternally on guard and destroy anything that tries to breach their perimeter.

Just what happened to Area-56, the personnel who were stationed there, or the powerful reality warping anomaly they contained, continues to be a mystery.

SCP-1451 has been classified as Euclid, and is considered to be effectively contained at its current location.

A sphere of wire mesh netting has been erected around it in order to ensure that no objects enter its activation area, but in the event that an object does manage to enter the circle, the statues are to be remotely monitored and no attempts whatsoever are to be made to try and rescue the person or object that triggered the Class 3 scenario.

8. SCP-031 NORTH KOREA HOTEL

A construction worker puts the final nail into the wall of the room he's working on.
He stands up and admires his work.
This is going to be a beautiful hotel one day, a true triumph for not just him, but
the entire country, and he's proud that he got to play a small part in its construction.
He starts to pack up his tools, there's plenty more rooms that need work.
It's a massive structure that will ultimately hold thousands.
What a modern marvel.
As he finishes putting away his tools, he notices something.
Through the still doorless frame, he sees someone walk by in the hallway.
Normally he wouldn't think anything of it, there's plenty of other people working on this floor of the hotel, but there's something about this woman… could it be?
No, it's not possible.
He takes out his wallet and opens it.
Inside is a faded photograph of the construction worker when he was still a young man, barely more than a boy really.
Standing next to him in the picture is the most beautiful woman he had ever known.

She was his first true friend, his best friend, and he always hoped that maybe it would turn into something more.

They grew up together, shared so many experiences, but then ultimately they were separated and lost touch.

He was never able to find her again, but as the picture in his wallet shows, he never stopped thinking about her.

Could it really be her though?

He runs into the hallway and calls out.

The woman stops at the end of the hallway and turns around.

She's carrying a tall stack of boxes that are blocking her face.

She sets them down and he sees... that it really is her!

They run towards each other, laughing like children, like the way they used to, and embrace in the middle of the hall.

He can't believe it, it's been so many years!

He never thought he would see her again.

How long has it been?

"Too long," she tells him.

He can't believe how little she's changed.

The years have hardly taken any toll on her, she's just as lovely and beautiful as that last day he saw her.

He asks her where she's been, what she's been doing, is she... married?

She tells him no, and that after they lost touch, she feels like she has just been looking for him, waiting for the day she would randomly see him pass by on the street, so that they could reconnect.

She just never thought it would happen that they'd be working in the same place at the same time.

The construction worker can't believe it either.

They both start to ask each other something at the same time, but then stop and laugh at speaking over each other.

"You go first" he tells her, "no you" she responds with a laugh.

Just then they're both interrupted by the sound of a whistle.

The work is finished for the day.

That's the signal to pack up and go home.

The construction worker tells her to wait there, he just has to go grab his tools and

then the two of them can go down together.

But as he turns to leave she reaches out and grabs his hand.

"Wait" she tells him.

He stops and turns back to her.

"It's ok" he tells her, "I'll be right back" but she doesn't seem to want to let go of his hand.

"Please, not yet" she tells him.

"I just want you to stay with me."

He looks down at his hand.

She's gripping him so tight that it starts to hurt a little.

"Really, I'll just be a second," he tells her, "then we can go somewhere and catch up."

But still she won't let go of his hand.

"I need you" she tells him.She steps close to him, pressing her body against his.

She closes her eyes and opens her mouth and he feels himself doing the same.

"I've always needed you…" she says as their mouths are about to meet.

"I need you forever."

The construction worker screams as the tiny tendrils emerge from the woman's body and plunge into his flesh.

He opens his eyes to see the girl he once knew morphing into a writhing mass of fibers, each reaching out towards him.

A long tentacle-like appendage wraps itself around his legs before whipping up and around his body, constraining him, as a second tentacle wraps around his head, stifling his screams, before popping his head off of his body.

North Korea… it's a country that's shrouded in mystery, whose government, culture, and day to day life is a black box to many foreigners.

But there's another secret inside, one that even the SCP Foundation is desperate to get to the bottom of, one that they know as SCP-031.

SCP-031 is a massive organism, estimated to weigh more than 7,500 kilograms, that can currently be found in a very surprising location… the Ryugyong Hotel which is located in Pyongyang, the capital of Democratic People's Republic of Korea.

The giant creature lives within the ductwork and maintenance infrastructure of the building where it has spread to all 105 floors of the hotel.

Each of its many tendrils ends in a pod-like growth called a sporocarp, which are approximately two meters in length and covered in many cilia-like structures.

Subjects have reported that when in the presence of these sporocarp, they don't see them as the writhing mass of organic matter that they really are, but rather as an individual from their past, often with one whom they shared an intense emotional attachment.

When taking this form, the sporocarp will try to convince the subject to remain with them for an extended period of time.

The sporocarp will then attempt to make physical contact with the subject, and if successful, its cilia-like structures will begin injecting digestive juices directly into the subject.

This will lead to the start of a process that will eventually cause their flesh to be broken down, consumed, and then incorporated into SCP-031's body mass.

Unfortunately for the victim, this horrific process does not kill them.

At the same time they are being digested, a flagellum, which is a tentacle-like appendage, will emerge from the sporocarp and wrap around the subject's head.

This flagellum has its own set of tiny tendrils that penetrate the cranial cavity and replace the victim's brain's blood vessels, which has the effect of keeping the brain alive and functioning.

The head is then removed from the body and the brain is transported to the central mass of the SCP-031 organism, where it too is incorporated into the creature.

It is estimated by Foundation researchers that SCP-031's mass contains thousands of such brains, and by all appearances, they are still alive… and conscious.

The Foundation first became aware of SCP-031 in 1948, following reports of police activity in North Korea at a location where multiple citizens had gathered near a refugee camp.

Those gathered were proclaiming their love for a cult-like leader they referred to as

"The Beloved."

The civilians were able to be calmed through the use of gas based tranquilizers and amnestics by Mobile Task Force Psi-7, who then recovered a mass that would later be known as SCP-031 and secured it at a local containment site.

The SCP-031 creature only weighed 75 kilograms at this time, and still had a vaguely human shape.

It did not seem to be able to incorporate other matter into its form at this point either, nor could it take on other people's forms, with its only anomalous effect seeming to be its ability to inspire intense feelings of love and devotion.

The breakout of the Korean War in 1950 led to the destruction of the Foundation containment site, and all anomalies housed there escaped.

Following the end of the war in 1953, all of the escaped anomalies were accounted for, all except SCP-031, which was presumed dead. Little more thought was given to the terminated anomaly until 1992, when the SCP Foundation caught wind of reports describing numerous fatalities involving workers at the Ryugyong Hotel.

A Mobile Task Force was sent to the hotel to investigate further, but after none of the members returned from the mission, the hotel was locked down and all construction was halted until further notice.

By 2008, the increased infestation of the still windowless hotel led to local officials starting construction again to finish the building's exterior and hopefully hide the presence of SCP-031 within, which led to the deaths of even more workers.

It's estimated that at its peak infestation, more than 75% of the hotel's 3,000 rooms were infested by SCP-031, but reclamation efforts have been able to reduce that number substantially.

Flame projecting equipment is able to destroy SCP-031 tendrils and sporocarps, as well as any personnel who have become assimilated into SCP-031.

Reclamation efforts are ongoing and local officials continue to work with the SCP Foundation to facilitate the ultimate containment or neutralization of the entity.

But there's one more strange twist to this story.

The more astute SCP experts may have noticed the similarities to SCP-1427, a large slab of beryllium bronze with mind altering effects that is also located within the Ryugyong Hotel.

How is it that two anomalies, both of which strongly impact the human brain, are both somehow housed at the same location?

Some clues exist in the form of a classified communication chain between two senior members of Foundation staff.

The two discuss the obvious discrepancies that exist when there are records of two anomalies both existing at the same place at the same time, with neither file referencing the other.

It leads to a strange paradox where for one to exist, the other isn't able to.

And yet, they both do exist.

Teams sent to investigate SCP-1427 will find SCP-1427, and teams sent to investigate SCP-031
will find SCP-031, and yet the first team will have no memory of seeing SCP-031, and vice versa.

When the teams were sent at the same time, they were unable to find each other, as if they were existing in parallel dimensions, each with its own version of the Ryugyong Hotel housing its own version of an SCP classified anomaly.

Do both anomalies exist?

Or perhaps neither of them do?

And both SCPs are in fact the result of a third, as yet unknown anomaly?

The answer to that question remains unknown, at least to the two senior members of staff who were communicating about the contradictory files.

Both were relieved of their duties under... well... suspicious circumstances, and for the time being, both files continue to exist in the database, just as both anomalies seem to exist in the Ryugyong Hotel.

For now, this Euclid class anomaly continues to be contained as well as it can be within the ducts and maintenance shafts of the Hotel's central spire.

The three secondary spires each contain a Type-9 Heaven's Blade Restriction System that focuses a disruptive energy field towards the central spire.

This system prevents SCP-031's psychic energies from escaping the structure and affecting any off-site personnel, as North Korean teams continue to push back against the spreading tendrils in the hopes that one day they will finally be able to open the hotel.

9. THE STARVING SKELETONS SCP-2863-GASHADOKURO

"The young couple held hands as they walked through the forest, the only light coming from the full moon which streamed down between the branches."

The young woman is riveted by her friend's story.

She's never been a fan of ghost stories, she scares too easily, but her friends insisted.

"But what they didn't know was that there was something else out there in the forest, something watching them."

The young woman can't help but look around, scanning the forest to see if there's anything out there watching her, but it's too dark to see anything past the dim ring of light cast by the campfire.

"Just then, something emerged from the forest.

The couple had no idea that it was just feet behind them, matching them step for step.

Slowly, it began to reach out towards them...

"What was it?" the young woman instinctually asked.

"It was...THE GASHADOKURO!"

The young woman screams in fear as she is grabbed from behind by a skeleton.

But of course the laughing of her friends clues her in immediately that this is not a real Gashadokuro, it's just her stupid friend in a mask.

No one can contain their laughter, even the young woman has to laugh a little.

As her friend takes off his cheap, skull mask she playfully hits him in the arm, "you jerk!"

"You should have seen the look on your - "

[NOTE: This is the big jump scare as the giant skeleton leaps out and immediately

grabs the boy who was wearing the mask Make sure the skeleton who first appears also steps on the campfire and puts it out.

Two of the others are immediately grabbed by another skeleton.

It's just the storyteller and the main girl who escape into the woods.

The skeletons are huge.

They can all vary in size but they should be around 300 feet tall]

The gigantic, shrieking skeleton leaps from the woods and picks up the young man, shoving him straight into his mouth and consuming him, the boy crying out as his bones are snapped between its enormous jaws.

Everyone screams and turns to run, but another colossal skeleton emerges from the forest, picking up two of the group, one in each hand, before smashing them together over and over, leaving nothing but a tenderized pile of flesh between its bony fingers that it then begins to devour.

The young woman doesn't know what to do.

She's petrified with fear, unable to move or even think.

She's grabbed from behind and turns to see her friend who was telling the story.

"Come on, we have to go!"

She still doesn't move, she can't tear herself away from watching the horror that's playing out in front of her, but he grabs her hand and forcefully pulls her into the forest behind him.

As they run through the woods, they can hear the sounds of their friends being eaten by the enormous skeletons.

There's nothing they can do to help them though, all they can do is run.

The two sprint as fast as they can through the thick, dark forest, jumping over fallen trees, hoping that there's solid ground on the other side.

The young woman's foot catches in a root and she falls hard to the ground.

Her friend stops and quickly comes back.

As he is helping her stand up out of the mud they both notice something.

A sound.

The heavy thuds of another giant skeleton.

And it's getting closer to them.

"Come on, we have to keep going!"

With a loud shriek, a huge bony hand emerges from the forest and grabs the young man.

The young woman watches as he is lifted a hundred feet into the air and stuffed whole into the gargantuan skeleton's mouth.

She steps slowly backwards, knowing that she will soon meet the same fate, until the earth disappears beneath her feet.

She tumbles down the hillside, somersaulting end over end, crashing through the brush on the hillside until dropping over embankment.

If the fall down the hill knocked her out then the drop over the embankment was enough to wake her back up.

Her wits come back just enough for her to roll under the embankment's ledge, and not a moment too soon.

She huddles under the ledge and watches as the two skeletons stride over her hiding place and continue on deeper into the forest.

She listens until the sounds of their thudding steps disappear.

She doesn't know what to do, should she try to get back to the campsite and see if

any of her friends are still alive?

If they are, they might need her help.

But what if there are more of these… things… out there?

What if they come back, looking for her?

Her mind races, unsure of what to do, and she has trouble thinking clearly.

Her ears are ringing from her tumble down the hillside and her teeth audibly chatter in fear.

As she debates her next move, trying to make sense of the nightmare she's found herself in, she suddenly notices something.

A shadow cast by the moonlight begins to grow on the ground in front of her.

That's when she realizes something else, it's not her teeth that are chattering.

The sound is coming from somewhere else.

She stands up and turns around to see a huge skull slowly rising up behind her.

The giant skeleton, this one even bigger than the others, reaches out towards her.

The girl closes her eyes, preparing to meet her fate as the skeleton starts to shriek.

But it's a different kind of sound.

She opens her eyes and is almost blinded by the intense white light on the skeleton's face.

It sounds like it is shrieking in pain from the light being cast on it, and she's forced

to turn away and shield her eyes.

As she does so, she sees the source of the light.

It's a man in a uniform.

He looks like some sort of tactical police officer, but instead of a gun, he's holding an enormous flashlight that he's pointing at the skeleton.

More men who are dressed just the same emerge from the woods, blasting the skeleton with more light.

It continues shrieking but seems helpless to do anything.

She watches as the skeleton seems to lose its form, slowly disintegrating in the light until eventually it disappears completely

Later, the young woman is sitting in the back of a van with a blanket wrapped around her shoulders.

One of the policemen, at least she thinks he must be a policeman, brings her a hot drink.

She still can't believe what she saw that night, the monstrous creatures that killed and ate her friends, it felt like it wasn't real, like she was watching a movie play out.

"Were those… were those Gashadokuro?" she asks.

A man in a white lab coat looks up from a nearby table where he had been working on something.

She thinks he must be a doctor of some kind.

"Yes," he tells her, "or something similar to them.

Maybe they inspired the myth of the Gashadokuro, maybe the myth inspired them.

We simply don't know."

She asks, "all my friends are - " "Dead" he interjects.

"I know this is hard for you, getting chased by giant anomalous skeletons and watching your friends eaten alive would be tough for anyone to deal with."

The young woman starts to sob, the weight of the moment finally hitting her.

"But I have some good news" he tells her.

She sniffs and looks up at the doctor.

"Believe it or not, I've seen this thing happen a lot, and you don't have to worry, because you're not going to remember any of this."

"Ouch" the young woman cries, and looks down to see that he has jabbed her in the thigh with a syringe.

She tries to push him away but she's already feeling weak and disoriented.

She sways a little before her eyes shut and she passes out.

The young woman wakes in the cheery morning light of her own bedroom.

She yawns and stretches, the strange dream about skeletons in the forest already drifting from her mind.

Konnichiwa!

I'm Dr. Max and today's file is a terrifying anomalous entity referred to in Japan as the Gashadokuro, but known by the SCP Foundation as SCP-2863... the Starving Skeletons.

SCP-2863 is not just one, but an entire population of entities that resemble gigantic human skeletons.

These enormous, bony creatures' size can vary, but on average they are approximately 30 meters tall.

While their exact number is unknown, over 200 separate individual instances have been identified and catalogued, with each having distinctive markings such as their bones having different types of damage or burn marks present.

SCP-2863 instances are currently found exclusively in Japan, where they will appear only after sunset.

It is still unknown if the skeletons are sapient, though they do appear sentient as they engage in their primary behavior of hunting down and consuming humans.

Despite their enormous size, they are capable of moving very quietly when they want to, though there have been reports from survivors of their appearance being preceded by a rattling like sound, which may be their own teeth or giant bones hitting against each other.

Once they have caught a human, they will immediately devour them, with the human's blood appearing to be absorbed directly into their bones, since they lack any digestive organs.

It is unknown if they require the blood of humans for sustenance, or if their predatory behavior is motivated by something else.

Monitoring and control of SCP-2863 instances was previously the responsibility of the Imperial Japanese Anomalous Matters Examination Agency.

The IJAMEA, which as the name suggests, was Imperial Japan's answer to the SCP Foundation, tasked with investigating the strange anomalies within their own borders for the benefit of the empire.

Several of the IJAMEA agents who had been investigating the Gashadokuro at the end of World War 2 transferred to the SCP Foundation when the Anomalous Matters Examination Agency was disbanded and continued their work on the anomaly.

They also provided their original files on the anomaly, which gave the Foundation their first information on the giant anomalous skeletons.

According to the IJAMEA's translated file:

"Gashadokuro are created by mass death, by the concentrated suffering of hundreds.

While the Gashadokuro will eventually fade, they remain for centuries after their creation, lingering until their sorrow has diffused and faded.

There is no way to hasten this process."

The IJAMEA file also explained that while conventional weaponry is useless against the anomalous skeletons, light can be used to banish the creatures, and either natural daylight or manmade light will suffice.

When exposed to light, the skeletons will start to lose their corporeal form until they fade away completely.

This doesn't kill instances of SCP-2863 though, it only temporarily neutralizes them, and appearances of the same instance will often be reported the very next night.

Just as the IJAMEA had noted in their file, the SCP Foundation also made the connection between SCP-2863 and locations of mass suffering.

While Imperial Japan's anomalous investigation unit identified 203 instances of SCP-2863, the Foundation has since become aware of three others, each of which were found at sites connected to death and destruction.

The first new instance was found near Nanjing, China, the location of an especially brutal massacre during the second world war that may have resulted in as many as 300,000 deaths.

It's believed that the entity first appeared in this location in 1938, just after the massacre, while the city was still under the control of Imperial Japan.

This has led some to speculate that the locations where Gashadokuro appear are inherently tied to the borders of Japan as a nation, and have fluctuated with geopolitical changes.

The second was discovered several kilometers from Fukuoka City in Japan, a city that saw heavy firebombing by Allied Forces during the war.

The third was identified in 2011 in the Tōhoku region of Japan, which is where the Fukushima nuclear disaster occurred.

Each of these new instances appeared to bear injuries consistent with someone who suffered through the nearby tragedies, with the first showing evidence of crushed bones, the second appearing to have suffered intense burning, and the third missing teeth which is common in cases of extreme radiation poisoning.

These specific injuries add further evidence of the connection the Gashadokuro may have to human misery.

The impermanent nature of SCP-2863 and their ability to manifest even after being neutralized has made long term containment of this anomaly all but impossible, and they have been classified as Keter.

In the event that an instance is spotted, Mobile Task Force Omicron-3 is dispatched to the area where they will attempt to neutralize the entity through the use of high-powered floodlights.

Any civilians who are exposed to SCP-2863 and survive are given Class-A amnestics so that they can hopefully move on with their lives and forget their horrifying encounter with the Starving Skeletons.

10. SCP-1500 PLANT VIRUS TAKES OVER BODY

ll unknown what kind of long term effects this exposure may have or how dangerous to their mental or physical health it will turn out to be.

Even more concerning, is that evidence has emerged that SCP-1500 may be able to affect more than just those in its immediate presence.

Recently, a United States Senator was giving a televised speech on a rather uninteresting topic.

The speech started out normal enough, but then the senator began to relay an anecdote about a childhood fishing trip he had taken with a friend.

You won't be surprised to learn that according to the senator, the friend's name was none other than Zachary Callahan.

Investigations into the senator's background concluded that there was no person by that name of the appropriate age in the area where he grew up.

It was also discovered the senator had suffered an especially bad migraine at a dinner party the week before the speech.

Further research into SCP-1500's memory altering effects have also revealed that they might just be more intrusive than first believed.

Rather than simply appearing as an old friend, subjects exposed to 1500 have begun to report that Zachary Callahan actually played a much more prominent role in their lives, either as a close relative, a parental figure, or even a former lover.

In each of these cases, the subjects described their feelings for Zachary Callahan as ones of adoration, and that he made them feel protected and loved.

Most troubling of all, is a recent addendum to the SCP-1500 file, which describes the very latest research on the anomaly and its effects.

It is now estimated that as many as 23,000 people all across the world have been affected by the creature, with the idea of Zachary Callahan implanted into their memories.

It is unknown why it is trying to spread its influence so far and wide, but one clue that may point to a nefarious purpose is that it seems to be disproportionately targeting political and military figures, as well as SCP Foundation personnel.

Following these new developments, classification of SCP-1500 to keter was requested and granted.

Due to the risk that SCP-1500 poses through its anomalous effects, and its powerful ability to influence those in positions of great power, it is permanently kept in a modified humanoid containment cell at Site-17.

No personnel are allowed to enter into its containment chamber under any circumstances, nor are there security cameras in its cell.

A false containment document describing a human male with an anomalous plant-like effect was placed in the database in order to deter further investigation into the real SCP-1500, and any personnel who experience painful, persistent headaches are immediately transferred away from Site-17, while any who attempt to breach containment are immediately terminated.

Is SCP-1500 planting the seeds for something big by infiltrating the minds of some of the most influential people on earth?

Or is it merely looking for a connection as it takes on a form that it wishes it could have in the only way it can, inside an imagination.

Perhaps one day, we will know the answer.

Now go and watch another entry from the files of Dr. Max, like SCP-1500, the story of me and my best friend Zach and the time we rode motorcycles across South East Asia... wait a second...

I didn't do that with Zach.

11. SCP-095-THE DEMON CORE

A scientist sits in his lab working on an experiment when the door suddenly opens and a tall, hard-nosed man enters.

The scientist hastily stands up and salutes the General who oversees the scientist's entire program.

The General dispenses with formalities and tells the scientist that he's being assigned to something new.

Before the scientist can even ask what it is he'll be working on, the General gives a small wave of his hand and two soldiers appear in the doorway.

They are each holding the side of a large metal box, and from the strained expression on their faces, it's clear that the box is very heavy.

They set the box down on the scientist's heavy wooden desk with a loud thud before stepping away from it.

The scientist looks over the bulky, lead case that's been brought to him, no idea of what could be waiting inside.

"Be very careful with this" the General says, before handing a folder full of papers to the scientist.

The scientist, unsure of how to respond, moves his hand to salute the General, but he has already turned on his heel and started to exit the small lab, followed closely behind by the two soldiers.

The scientist looks over the folder that was given to him.

There's nothing on the cover so he opens it and starts looking inside, skimming over the long, dry paragraphs that say nothing at all and seem to be included in every government report for some reason.

Ah, there it is.

Contents.

One 6.2 kilogram sphere of…

Plutonium 239.

Plutonium 239?!

He's been doing research in this Army run research lab for some time and knows exactly what this is.

A sphere of plutonium 239 can only be one thing… a core for a new atomic bomb.

Two were already dropped on the cities of Hiroshima and Nagasaki, and their never before seen power caused death and destruction on a truly horrendous level.

But they had also helped to put an end to the second world war, potentially saving the lives of thousands or even millions more.

And no matter what moral questions he had about it, this was his job, and as an expert in physics and chemistry, his research would potentially help put a stop to fighting in the future.

After all, no one would dare go to war when they knew their opponent had weapons that could cause devastation on this scale, right?

The scientist pours over the typewritten reports, reading each and every handwritten note in the margins.

As he reads through them, he sees warnings about the experiments from the report's unnamed author.

There are references to how slim the safety margins are when handling the material for testing.

Since the core is intended to be used in a new nuclear weapon, it needs to be right on the edge of supercriticality, the point where fissile material undergoes a chain reaction that is key to nuclear detonations.

The report then describes an experiment where the core was to be surrounded with bricks made of tungsten carbide that would act as a mirror of sorts, bouncing neutrons back at the core, which would knock loose other neutrons.

The experiment was to be stopped before the core went supercritical, but when the scientist turns the page to view the results he finds… nothing.

There's no more pages in the folder.

The scientist had heard rumors about these types of experiments.

Tickling the dragon's tail they called it.

But where were the rest of the reports?

Was this really the last experiment that was done?

He sees at the top of the page that this last experiment was performed over a year ago.

Just then the scientist notices someone walking by in the hall.

It's the general!

He runs out into the hallway waving the report at him.

"General, general!"

The general stops and turns around, clearly annoyed at being intercepted while on the way from one important meeting to another.

"General, what happened in the last experiment?"

The General somehow looks even more annoyed by the question.

"Don't worry about it" he barks back at the scientist.

"His time on the project was finished.

It's yours now."

And with that, the general leaves the scientist standing in the hall with his incomplete file.

Days pass and the scientist receives additional orders on what types of experiments he should be carrying out.

All of them are designed to guarantee that the core of plutonium will be suitable for use in a new weapon.

For the latest test, he's performing an experiment not dissimilar to the last one described in the report, but instead of using tungsten carbide bricks to reflect neutrons back at the core and achieve criticality, a beryllium dome had been created which is to be lowered down over the sphere of plutonium.

As he lowers the dome, he knows that if it were to close completely, it would cause the core to go supercritical in an instant.

In order to prevent this, he uses a screwdriver to prop up one side of the dome, allowing just enough neutrons to escape so that the core can maintain its stability.

As he lowers the dome just a small amount more, he starts to hear something.

It's a faint noise at first, but gradually grows more and more audible.

Radioactivity produces no sound, so the scientist is confused, especially since it sounds like the noise is coming from inside the dome.

But surely that's impossible.

There were no processes happening within that should be creating any sort of noise.

The scientist bends down and lifts up the edge of the dome ever so slightly more, just enough so that he can peek inside.

As he does, the sound grows louder.

He looks right into the core of plutonium 239 and sees something.

There is movement on the sphere.

He knows this is impossible, but he can see them with his own eyes, images dancing on the surface of the plutonium sphere.

They were faces, unnatural faces, contorted and twisted in pain.

He can see now that these are the source of the sound he was hearing, because the faces… are screaming.

The scientist jumps back and the screwdriver slips away from the edge of the beryllium dome, allowing it to fall and completely cover the plutonium.

Out in the hallway, a security guard covers his eyes, momentarily blinded by the flash of intense, blue light.

When his vision returns, he runs into the laboratory it came from.

The exposed sphere of plutonium sits on the desk, and the security guard looks up to see that the dome that once covered it has been embedded into the ceiling.

He hears a moan come from the other side of the desk and rushes around to help the scientist, but when he looks down at the ground he doesn't see a man.

Lying there on the floor is a charred and bloody body, the small amount of skin and flesh that is left sloughing off his body.

The scientist reaches towards him with a skeletal hand, emitting one final groan before collapsing.

Nuclear weapons have claimed many lives, not just those who suffered directly from their overwhelming destructive energy or the subsequent residual radiation known as fallout, but many of those who researched and developed the science and technology behind them also became victims of their incredible, almost otherworldly power.

Today's anomaly is an example of exactly that, combining the astonishing power of nuclear weapons with the world of the supernatural.

This is SCP-095-FR...

The Demon Core.

SCP-095-FR, is a 6.2 kilogram sphere, 89 millimeters in diameter that is composed entirely of plutonium 239.

Despite at one point seeming to be a normal sphere of the plutonium isotope, SCP-095-FR now seems to be in a permanent self-sustaining state of criticality.

This results in a near constant emission of alpha radiation which is powerful enough to damage any electrical circuits within a 20 meter radius.

The sphere's danger grows the closer you get to it too.

Within a 10 meter radius, any living tissue will become extremely irradiated, leading to radiation sickness, while denser materials like metal or bone will themselves become extremely radioactive.

The plutonium sphere is somehow able to maintain a consistent mass despite its state which should lead to a decrease in overall mass.

It's theorized that it may be undergoing some kind of regenerative process, though it's been impossible to determine just how this might be occurring.

SCP-095-FR was recovered from the seafloor near Bikini Atoll, which was the site of a series of nuclear weapon tests by the United States government known as Operation Crossroad.

These and later tests including the Castle Bravo test resulted in the island chain becoming extremely irradiated, and many of the island's residents soon showed signs of acute radiation syndrome leading to much of the indiginous population being forced to relocate.

Following the Operation Crossroad test, an anomalously high source of radiation was detected in the sea.

Though records are incomplete, it appears that the core of plutonium that had been responsible for the deaths of multiple scientists had somehow ended up on the ocean floor.

Whether it got there due to being part of a failed bomb detonation, or if it somehow appeared there by other, more anomalous means is unknown.

But regardless of how it got there, the attempted recovery of the object led to the deaths of several American servicemembers from radiation related illnesses, which the SCP Foundation soon learned of.

After assisting in the retrieval of the sphere, the plutonium was relinquished to the Foundation's custody for containment.

The SCP-095-FR sphere was placed under the purview of the French Branch of the SCP Foundation, owing to their having a readily available site for containment, where the sphere was stored in a lead lined, radiation blocking safe and classified as Euclid.

Only D-Class were permitted to transport and handle the plutonium since its effects amounted to a death sentence for anyone who got too close.

They were also responsible for transferring the sphere to a new safe every six months due to the damage it was causing them from constant bombardment of radiation.

All of these containment procedures would have to be changed though, following the events of January 7th, 2015.

On that day, sixty-nine years after it first took the lives of two scientists at the Los

Alamos laboratory, and despite it being a scientific impossibility, the Demon Core suddenly went supercritical all on its own.

The resulting explosion was estimated to be roughly thirty-three kilotons, or about twice the power of the atomic bombs that had been detonated over Hiroshima and Nagasaki.

Nearly the entire site housing SCP-095-FR was destroyed along with fourteen other Safe and Euclid class anomalies, and in the end, the death count totalled 285, with casualties coming from either the blast itself, the collapse of structures on the site, or from the resulting radiation poisoning.

Incredibly, the sphere itself survived the explosion, showing no signs that it had detonated with the force of a nuclear weapon when it was recovered from the site's wreckage.

Foundation researchers studying the Demon Core determined that it was likely to explode again in roughly fifty years, and that the only discernible difference measured in the core before it suddenly went supercritical and destroyed the Foundation site was a sudden spike in radiation.

Foundation scientists have no idea how the Demon Core survived, or how it detonated without warning.

Some theorize that it may exist in some kind of time loop, which would potentially explain its explosion-regeneration cycle, and that it is possible the core has actually detonated several times before entering into Foundation custody.

But perhaps the bigger question when it comes to the Demon Core and why it has become such a dangerous object... is why.

Is there something contained within this seemingly cursed sphere of plutonium?

Is a part of those who have been impacted by the quest to harness the power of atomic energy somehow contained within?

Now desperate to get out and unleash their anger on the world?

Research continues, but due to the extreme danger that comes from working with the anomaly, it's likely these questions will remain unanswered for some time.

Following the destruction of the Foundation site, SCP-095-FR was reclassified to Keter, and moved to an underground bunker designed to withstand an explosion equivalent to a standard atomic bomb, which it is hoped will be enough to contain the blast that is almost inevitably going to happen again.

It's a sobering thought, even for those of us who work with and around anomalies on a daily basis, to be reminded of the incredible destructive power of nuclear weapons.

Some of the most feared and deadly anomalies contained by the SCP Foundation pale in comparison to the carnage that we've inflicted on ourselves, and it's important to remember that sometimes the true demons are found inside of us.

12. SCP-2710   TRUE   SOLITARY CONFINEMEN

A prisoner in a striped uniform is led down the central corridor of a penitentiary by a pair of guards.

Wherever he's being taken, the prisoner is not going peacefully.

The other inmates stand at their cell doors watching as he is dragged past them.

The prisoner is begging for the guards to show him mercy, pleading for them not to make him go in there, to subject him to anything, anything in the world but that.

The guards pay no attention to his cries as they force him along.

They reach the end of the corridor and stop in front of the last cell. Number 667.

The prisoner looks into the dark, empty cell and screams, struggling against his captors one last time before they overpower him and shove him inside, slamming the door shut behind him.

The prisoner looks around the small, dim cell.

All that's inside is a bed with a thin mattress and a filthy toilet.

He looks extremely scared, his eyes searching around the cell as if a monster is going to leap out from a dark corner and grab him.

The prisoner hears a cracking sound and jumps in fright, spinning around to see a different kind of monster.

Standing between the two guards who led him here, is a third prison guard.

He's enormous, and the prisoner watches as he cracks the knuckles of his massive hands.

The giant guard reaches for something hanging next to the cell door. It's a… clipboard.

He looks at the prisoner's uniform and notes his name before writing it down.

The large guard asks over his shoulder "so… what are we thinking? One day?

Two?"

"For this one?" one of the other guards answers, "he deserves a lot more than that for what he did."

"Why, what'd he do?" asks the big one.

"He attacked one of the nurses.

She's in pretty bad shape."

"One of the nurses?" the veins in the larger guard's head start to bulge out as
his grip on the pencil tightens.
"Who was it?"
"It was… it was Gloria" the guard answers.
The pencil snaps in the giant guard's hand.
One of the guards quickly picks it up and hands it back to him.
Through gritted teeth he answers "I see…"
As the giant guard stares at him with angry, violent eyes, the prisoner starts to slink back into the dark cell, terrified of what's going to happen to him.
"You like to attack nurses, do ya?
Well we're going to give you plenty of time to think about it.
I'll see you… in a year."
The two other guards look at each other, clearly thinking that this is extreme even for a crime like this.
"Are you sure that's a good idea?" one of them asks, but it's already too late.
The guard has penciled in the date for exactly one year later.
"No, please no!" the prisoner screams, rushing towards the bars and reaching out
as if it will somehow help him, but it doesn't.
There is a faint rustling of wind that seems to carry the sound of whispers, and then… the prisoner vanishes.
He's simply gone, blinked out of existence.
The guard hangs the clipboard back on the wall before turning and quickly walking away.
He needs to get to the infirmary.
The two guards can do nothing but shrug at each other and follow after him.
"Poor guy" one of them whispers as they walk away from the empty cell.
One year to the day later, the huge guard walks down the same prison corridor.
It's late at night, and as he walks along he lets his baton hit against the bars of the cells, making a loud clatter.
"Wake up everyone, wake up.
It's a homecoming day."
Sleepy prisoners get up out of their beds and stand at the front of their cells, trying
their best to look through the bars to see the cell at the end of the block.

"See what happens when you mess with staff.

Come on, get up, get up.

Today's the day.

It's a homecoming!"

The guard gets to the end of the corridor and stops in front of the empty cell with

the clipboard hanging on the wall next to it.

The door is open and there's nothing inside the dark cell except for the same dirty toilet and bed.

The guard takes out his pocket watch and checks the time.

Everyone, the guard and the prisoners alike, are all focused on the empty cell.

The guard checks his watch again.

The minute hand ticks over to midnight, and the moment it does the cell door slides shut and locks with a loud click.

The prison is completely silent, each inmate waiting with bated breath to see what happens next.

The guard takes out a large, heavy ring of keys and inserts one into the cell door before stepping inside.

He looks around and still it appears that nothing inside is different.

But then he spots what he's looking for.

There in the corner, near the toilet, is a huddled figure in a striped prison uniform.

"Well well well, there you are."

The guard starts to walk towards this person who has somehow appeared in the cell, but the huddled figure doesn't move or react in any way.

The guard reaches down and puts a hand on the man to flip him over "How'd you enjoy your stay?"

Solitary confinement is one of the most brutal forms of punishment that is still in use across much of the world today.

The psychological and physical distress that comes from days, weeks, months, even sometimes years spent alone can be devastating.

But as horrible as this practice is, there exists a form of retribution that is even more terrifying.

One that even the most hardened of criminals fear and would do anything to avoid.

This is SCP-2701, also known as…

True Solitary.

SCP-2701 is a seemingly standard looking prison cell located in a now condemned Pennsylvania state penitentiary.

The prison, which was built in the early-mid 1800s, was showing its age long before it was finally shut down, and the cell contains only an old toilet and bed, with a clipboard hanging to the left of the cell with various forms marked as "Intake".

The cell's construction materials appear normal and the contents themselves are non-anomalous.

It is only when someone is placed inside of SCP-2701 and the clipboard next to the cell is used, that its frightening effects become evident.

When a human being is locked within the cell, their name is written on the intake form, and a date is filled in under the "release date" section, SCP-2701's anomalous activation event is put in motion.

Thirteen seconds after these conditions have been met, the person inside will disappear, completely vanishing from view as if they simply no longer exist.

Any attempts to better understand the process by which they dematerialize have been unsuccessful, as all recording equipment looking into or placed inside the cell will show only static or blank images during the thirteen seconds before the subject disappears.

Researchers observing the effect in person though, have reported the sounds of wind and unidentified whispering voices, but it is still unknown what may be producing these.

At 12:00am on the dot on the release date, the cell's door will somehow close and lock itself if it is not already shut.

At this exact moment, the person who vanished will reappear within the locked cell.

Unfortunately for the person who was locked inside, while they may have returned to our reality, it is unlikely that they will ever be the same.

Experiments into SCP-2701 have revealed that those who are placed inside and vanish will experience a state of complete sensory deprivation, while remaining fully conscious the entire time.

They experience no sounds, smells, or sense of touching anything.

They do not even see darkness, since that would imply sight.

Instead they truly experience no senses at all.

This effect can be disastrous for the human psyche, with subjects reporting that they have developed intense fears of both shadows and light, claustrophobia, agoraphobia, and a fear of going to sleep following their time within SCP-2701.

At the same time, they will have experienced no physical changes at all, including aging, no matter how much time has passed.

But the worst part of SCP-2701, is that those who are locked inside do not experience time at the same rate as you or I.

No, tests have revealed that once someone disappears from within the cell, they will feel as if time has been significantly stretched out, with the dilation effect causing them to perceive time at a rate that has been estimated to be between three and four hundred times longer than normal.

That means that someone placed inside for two hours will experience time as if they had been locked away for 25 to 33 days, while someone placed inside for a whole year will feel as though they have been floating in a void of nothingness for several centuries.

Foundation researchers have theorized that the absence of any outside stimulation for that long of a period causes the mind to break down rational thought structures in an effort to mitigate stress, and that a complete psychological breakdown soon follows.

In order to better understand the effects of SCP-2701, the SCP Foundation embarked on a number of tests using Class D personnel.

In one experiment, which was performed on a D-Class known as D-77391, the event started at 11:45pm and the release date was set for the coming midnight.

This led to the D-Class being inside the cell for fifteen minutes, though they experienced their time within as having lasted 75 to 100 hours.

When D-77391 was interviewed six hours after reappearing, they described their time inside as being a true hell.

Experiencing nothing but emptiness, they couldn't do anything.

They couldn't sleep, they couldn't even scream, they were left alone with only their thoughts and memories.

The only thing that kept them from completely losing their mind was something one of the researchers told them before they entered the cell.

The researcher told them that no matter what they felt, that they had to hold on to the idea that they were going to come back.

They needed to remember they wouldn't be in there forever.

While these words of encouragement did seem to stave off the worst of the mental effects D-77391 could have suffered, they also impacted the results of the experiment, and the offending researcher was later reassigned to a different project following a six-month suspension.

The SCP Foundation first became aware of SCP-2701 following reports of certain abnormalities at a Pennsylvania State Penitentiary.

There were numerous complaints by lawyers that they were not being allowed to meet with their clients, and that they were being denied access to the site by the prison's warden.

When police were finally dispatched to the site to investigate, it was discovered that the entire prison, which previously housed 137 inmates and employed a number of staff, had only one inhabitant - the warden.

He described the activation procedure for Cell 667, and explained that he had placed every single prisoner inside, one by one, and made them disappear.

He had been keeping the funds that were supposed to be used for the care of the inmates as well as to bribe officials and former staff, in order to keep the warden's scheme secret and prevent any official inquiries.

The warden surrendered to the police without incident, and an undercover Foundation agent within the Philadelphia police soon alerted SCP agents to the cell's anomalous effects.

When a Foundation team arrived on site, they found the cell exactly as described, along with the intake forms.

The prison warden had been telling the truth.

Over a hundred forms were filled out with inmate's names, with release dates ranging from fifty to over thirteen hundred years in the future.

The ease with which SCP-2701 is able to be contained, has led to it receiving the Safe classification.

The former prison where SCP-2701 is located is monitored at all times by video and audio surveillance, and a security guard equipped with full-body restraints is present at all times to both detain any subjects who appear within the cell, as well as prevent any new ones from being placed inside, that aren't a part of an official SCP Foundation experiment.

13. SCP-867 BLOOD SPRUCE

What was that?"

The man and woman's hike through a gently rolling portion of the Rocky Mountains has just taken a turn for the dangerous.

"There's something there in the bush" the man tells her before stepping in front of her in a defensive pose.

They watch the bush intently, there's a slight rustling of the leaves as if something is inside.

The man picks up a stick from the ground and holds it in front of him, ready to strike whatever fearsome beast is lurking in the underbrush.

The rustling stops but the man doesn't move from his protective stance.

"Do you think it's gone?" the woman asks.

The man isn't sure.

He leans in towards the bush, searching for signs of what might be hiding inside when

- Ahhh!

The man screams and falls backwards as the creature emerges from the bush.

"Aww" the woman cries, "it's a pika!"

She kneels down to get a closer look at the adorable little creature.

Pikas are native to this part of Colorado and they resemble rabbits but with small, rounded ears.

She watches it hop back off the trail before turning around to see her friend lying tangled in the branches of a tree.

She can't help but laugh as she offers a hand to help pull him out of his predicament.

"Are you alright?" she asks between fits of laughter.

Yes, he's fine.

The only thing hurt was his pride.

He notices a small red spot on his arm and rubs it, but it doesn't seem to hurt at all.

His attention is diverted by the woman though, who is marveling at the tree he was just stuck in.

Free of the branches, he can appreciate now that the tree really is incredible.

It looks like a huge blue spruce, but the name is a complete misnomer, because this tree is a vibrant red color.

"I've never seen anything like it," she says and the man hasn't either.

Neither knows what species it is, and strangely, there don't seem to be any others like it.

Maybe this is the result of an odd genetic defect that turns blue spruces red?

After admiring the tree for a moment, the pair decides that they've hiked far enough and that they should probably head back to the car. She jokes that he's likely exhausted from his run-in with a wild animal and he laughs, but clearly his ego has been bruised.

The man stops his car in front of the woman's house and she thanks him for taking her on the hike.

As she starts to get out though he stops her.

He asks if she wants to go do something else.

Like… dinner?

The woman thanks him for his offer, but she has to be up early the next day for work.

Just a quick drink then?

An hour?

30 minutes?

The woman tries her best to let her friend down easy, explaining that she likes him as a friend and as only that.

The man opens his mouth to respond but she stops him.

If he valued their friendship then he wouldn't try to take advantage of it by using it as a backdoor to dating her.

The man again looks like his pride has been shattered.

He apologizes and admits that she is right.

It's just that he has such a good time with her that he never wants it to end.

She gives him a sad smile as she closes the car door and he watches her enter her house before he finally drives away.

It's two weeks later when the man's phone rings.

It's his friend.

She explains that she's been thinking a lot about what he said in the car and that she likes spending time with him too.

Maybe there could be something more to their relationship.

The man can't believe it, is this really happening?

The woman is serious.

She'd like to take him up on that dinner offer if he's still interested, her treat.

She wants to know what he is doing right - AHH.

The man suddenly yelps in pain.

Is he okay?

What was that sound?

"Yes, I'm fine, it was nothing," the man tells her.

"It's just that now… now's not a good time."

The woman doesn't understand, she thought he'd want to see her.

She explains that she's leaving town for a work trip the next day and will be gone for a couple of weeks.

She was hoping she could see him before she left but - The man cries out in pain again.

He tells her that he hasn't been feeling well all day, but that he'll be alright.

"Okay, well… get well soon.

I'll call you when I get back."

They exchange goodbyes and the man hangs up the phone.

The man looks terrible.

His skin is pale and his face looks hollow and gaunt.

He looks down at his arm and sees that the veins themselves appear to be moving, pulsing and vibrating.

He screams again in agony and falls to the floor, clutching his arm.

After writhing on the floor he manages to summon the strength to reach for the phone.

His hand searches on the table above him and eventually he's able to knock it onto the floor.

He grabs the phone and starts to dial…

Nine…

One… before he can press one again another wave of intense searing pain consumes him.

Several weeks later, the woman is standing outside the man's house.

Mail and newspapers are piled up on his front porch, as if no one has been in or out in some time.

She knocks on the door but there's no response.

"Hello?" she calls out, but still nothing.

She's very worried.

She's tried calling him several times but he never answered or returned her messages.

She tries the doorknob and to her surprise, the front door swings open.

She steps inside and the room is dark.

She's also immediately hit by a strong aroma of… pine?

She searches on the wall and finds the switch.

She turns on the lights and can't believe what she sees standing in front of her.

There in the middle of the room, is a massive spruce tree, it's upper branches pressing against the ceiling.

She reaches out and touches the tree's vivid red branches.

They feel sticky and wet.

She pulls her hand away and looks down to see that it's covered in a red substance.

That's when she notices something else.

Stuck among the trunk at the base of the tree, is the half consumed body of her friend.

Unfortunately this pair would never have the opportunity to see their feelings take root and grow, because unbeknownst to them, this beautiful tree is actually a very deadly anomaly, known to the SCP Foundation as SCP-867, but which is perhaps better known by its very appropriate nickname...

Blood Spruce.

SCP-867 is, or at least appears to be, quite similar to the species of tree Picea pungens, better known as the blue spruce.

Of course there are a number of dramatic differences between 867 and its non-anomalous counterpart.

Visually, and most obvious, is the coloration.

While blue spruces, as the name implies, are typically a blue-green color, SCP-867 is a deep, vibrant red.

There's another major visual difference too, with the Blood Spruce lacking any sort of seed cones that you would normally expect to find.

With no pine cones to protect and spread seeds, you'd be right to ask how SCP-867 goes about reproducing.

The answer to that question is what makes this beautiful tree such a dangerous anomaly.

The secret to how SCP-867 reproduces is found in its leaves.

While they look like pine needles, SCP-867's leaves are, in fact... needles.

Their structure is very similar to that of hypodermic needles, and each one contains

a single long, thin seed which sits above a small gas pocket at the base.

When a living creature touches the leaves, the tree immediately reacts.

It triggers the gas pocket in the base of the leaf to release which injects the seed into the skin of whatever touched it.

The process is quite similar to that found in auto-injectors, like those used to quickly treat allergic reactions.

The seed itself is extremely small, and is coated in a liquid that has both anesthetic and coagulant properties, which makes the process virtually undetectable.

Once implanted in the skin, these seeds can lay dormant for up to two weeks, before they begin the germination process , and the true horror of SCP-867 is revealed.

Once the seeds begin to sprout and grow, they will not seek to penetrate through the skin like a plant rising out of the soil.

Instead, the strange plant will grow within its host's body, spreading throughout the circulatory system.

This process is extremely painful for the host.

The plant's tendrils wind through their veins and capillary system, stretching and pressing against them as the blood spruce grows within them.

Eventually, the ever increasing size of the plant's tendrils becomes too much and the veins will begin to rupture.

This leads to severe internal bleeding and soon after, the death of the host.

The entire process is quite quick, with it only taking twenty-four hours from when the seeds first sprout to the host dying, but that single day will feel like an eternity to the afflicted individual as they feel the plant rapidly growing inside of their body.

But even though the host has expired, this parasitoid tree is far from finished with them, or at least their body.

Soon after death, a new instance of the Blood Spruce will burst from the body.

The red tree is quite small at first, but it will continue to quickly grow, just as it did within its host's body, and can reach maturity in just thirty days.

And unlike most other plants, SCP-867 is able to grow regardless of light or soil conditions, because it does not produce food via photosynthesis, no this plant is carnivorous.

As it grows, the 867 will slowly consume its host's body until nothing remains except the blood red tree.

Instances of SCP-867 were first identified in Colorado during the 1990s, following reports of numerous disappearances of hikers and Park Rangers.

The SCP Foundation dispatched a team to the area to investigate, and they soon discovered numerous instances of the previously unidentified tree.

Several still young specimens were acquired, though unfortunately this led to the deaths of several agents, who were not yet aware of just how dangerous the red spruces could be.

Once their threat level was properly assessed, several specimens were flagged for containment and research purposes, while all of the other identified instances still in the wild were destroyed.

The remaining instances of SCP-867 were classified as Euclid, and are now securely kept at a Foundation Bio-Containment site.

Direct human contact with the plants is normally not allowed, and remote rovers are used for the majority of tests and upkeep.

If for any reason, it is necessary for a human to enter 867's containment cell, they are to wear full hazmat suits with a kevlar underlayer, and upon exiting the cell must undergo a full herbicidal treatment and inspection.

Should any possible puncture marks be discovered, they will be forced to quarantine for no less than fifteen days.

Ah nature…

It's so beautiful, peaceful, and calming, yet seems determined to try and kill us in any number of ways.

If you're out hiking or camping in the woods, try to remember this extremely famous adage which I may, or may not, have just made up.

It goes, "leaves of three, let them be, needles of red, well… you're probably already dead."

14. TORTURED IRON SOUL SCP-203

The group of children on their bikes stare intently at the large, abandoned house.

Rumors have been circulating all school year about a monster that lives inside.

One child tells the others about the kid from a couple towns over who went inside and never came back out and it's easy to believe that something evil could be lurking inside the rundown home with its peeling paint and many broken windows.

The children begin teasing each other, daring one another to go in and see the monster for themselves.

No one seems especially eager to volunteer though as they all egg each other on.

As the group of children joke about who should be forced to go inside, another comes riding up behind them, struggling to catch his breath.

"You left me behind again," he complains.

Clearly this is not the first time that this smallest child of the group has been made to try and keep up with his bigger and faster friends.

The bigger kids all turn to look at him.

They don't need to discuss it any further, the answer to who must go inside has already been decided.

The smaller child tries to protest, but ultimately, what decision does he have but to go inside?

He can't let everyone else think that he's a chicken, he's got to prove once and for all that he's just as tough as any of them.

Without another word he lets his bike fall into the dirt and makes his way towards the big, creepy house.

The door pushes open without any resistance and the boy looks into the dark house.

The boy steps inside and the floorboards creak loudly under his feet.

The inside looks much like the outside, old, worn, and abandoned.

01:24

But then he hears something, a scratching noise coming from above him.

He turns to leave but he can see all of his friends through the doorway, and they motion for him to keep going.

The boy steels his nerves and turns back, he's going to show them just how brave he is.

The boy starts up the stairs, each one groaning as he steps onto it.

He reaches the top of the stairs to find a landing with more rooms, each full of dirt and debris.

There's spray paint on many of the walls and lots of trash.

It looks like teens may use this as a place to hangout.

But there at the other of the landing is one more room.

And the door is shut.

From outside, the group of children can see through the upper windows as the boy makes his way through the house.

They're not laughing and teasing any longer, in fact they're impressed by how bravely he is exploring the old home.

Though none of them would admit it out loud, he's earning their respect.

The boy reaches the shut door at the end of the hall and presses his ear to it but he

doesn't hear anything inside.

He places his hand on the doorknob and slowly opens it.

The boy screams and falls backwards as the cat that was hiding inside panics and jumps through one of the open windows.

The boy can't help but laugh.

Of course it was just a - The boy screams again as the floor gives way beneath him and he crashes down onto the first floor in a pile of debris.

He's stunned by the fall before starting to scream again as that floor gives way too.

His yelling is silenced by the air being knocked out of him as he hits the basement floor.

He's covered in dust and pieces of two floors he fell through.

He feels bruised and sore, but he can wiggle his fingers and toes.

He's not paralyzed, and it doesn't even feel like he's broken a bone. Maybe he's okay.

But no, he's definitely not okay, because suddenly there's something picking him up off the floor.

As his eyes adjust to the dark basement, he sees what it is that's holding him - it's half man half machine, a huge, disgusting mix of metal and flesh.

The boy is too scared to scream any more as the creature's unmoving, dead looking eyes stare straight into his.

It's face looks as though the skin has been stretched across a human metallic skull. The boy can only watch as the monster raises its sharp, metallic fingers and... brushes the dirt out of the boy's hair.

The boy starts to whimper, but whatever this thing is, it doesn't seem to want to hurt him.

A tinny robotic voice coming from a small device on the creature's face suddenly breaks the silence.

هل أنتَ على ما يُرام؟

The boy doesn't understand, but the robotic man tilts his horrific head to the side and repeats the same thing.

The boy is still confused, but he feels like the robot is trying to tell him something.

He somehow gets the sense that it's not going to hurt him.

Is this the monster that everyone has been afraid of?

A misunderstood machine-man living down here in the basement?

The robotic flinches as something is smashed on the back of his head.

He tosses the boy to the side and turns to see the boy's friends, each of them armed with pieces of wood and other scraps as weapons.

They've come here to save their friend from the monster that they dared him to find.

Another runs up to strike the robot but before he can reach him, he falls to his knees in pain, as do the rest of the children.

The creature has begun emitting a high frequency noise and the children try to cover their ears.

They all feel a searing pain that makes it feel as though their heads will explode.

The piercing noise continues to ring out, but the monster looks like it has entered some kind of dormant state and is no longer moving.

The small boy is able to slowly get back to his knees, hands still clasped to the side of his head, and stand up.

He runs past the monster and his friends who are writhing on the floor in pain, up the stairs, and out of the old house.

A woman stands at a kitchen counter, chopping vegetables for their dinner that evening, and talking to her oldest daughter about her plans for that weekend when the back door suddenly bursts open.

Standing there is her son, the small boy.

He's barely able to whisper the words "monster... there's a monster in the basement" before he collapses, blood pouring from his ears and nose, before he begins convulsing on the floor.

At the local police station, an officer is speaking on the phone.

"I see.

Yes, that is quite strange.

A metal man?

You don't say.

I'll send someone out there right away, don't go anywhere."

The police officer hangs up the phone and looks around, making sure no one is nearby or listening to him, and then takes out a cell phone.

He dials a number from memory and someone answers on the other end almost immediately.

"Yes this is Field Agent Patch," the police officer says, "you need to get a containment team out here right away.

And a good one too.

I don't know what it is, but it's dangerous."

An SCP Foundation Mobile Task Force that specializes in containing dangerous humanoid threats soon arrived at the house and took the anomaly into captivity.

Misinformation teams concocted a cover story about a gas leak leading to the unfortunate deaths of several of the town's children and administering amnestics to any potential witnesses.

Once the messy business of containment was over though, it was time to figure out just what this strange creature was.

SCP-203 appears to have at one time been a Caucasian human male, though its appearance now is far different than it once was.

This bipedal humanoid creature stands 2.5 meters tall and weighs roughly 200 kilograms.

Both its incredible height and weight are due to the fact that the man's original skeleton has been entirely removed, and replaced with a mechanical framework made of cast iron.

The metal skeleton is much larger than the original bones, and in many places SCP-203's skin has split from being stretched over it, revealing the mechanical structure underneath.

Other parts of the framework appear to have been intentionally made to protrude through the skin, though it is unclear for what purpose.

In addition to this larger than normal mechanical skeleton, a number of other augmentations are present on SCP-203.

Its fingers have been extended into sharpened, hook-like barbs that are approximately 1 meter long.

Its lips have been removed entirely, making it clear that there is no movable jaw bone, and that the skull is likely one large hollow piece of metal, and there are several more hook-like protrusions jutting out around the mouth area, smaller but similar in appearance to the fingers.

SCP-203's legs have been modified as well, with two added joints that give them an appearance more akin to a dog's, and its toes have been removed and replaced with a solid piece of metal similar to those found in steel toed boots.

It's chest has no sternum or breastplate, which causes the skin stretched across to pull inward as its diaphragm contracts.

Its ears have also been removed, though it still seems to possess hearing that is far beyond that of an average human, and while its eyes still remain, they are held in a permanently forward facing position by several needles that emerge from the eye sockets.

The irises also appear permanently dilated and do not react to light.

In place of a mouth is a small speaker covered by a metal grate that is capable of producing basic vocalizations, though with a distinctly robotic sound to them.

Tests have shown that SCP-203 has a basic understanding of English, but its own primary language seems to be a type of Arabic, though there are no records of the exact dialect.

SCP-203 does not need to eat or drink, and without any visible mouth, it is likely incapable of either.

Instead it runs off of a power cell located within its body, that will provide energy for up to 72 hours.

After those three days, SCP-203 will shut down and enter a hibernation state for 3 to 4 hours during which its power source will recharge, providing it with another 72 hours of energy.

All attempts to examine SCP-203 by either X-ray, CT, ultrasound, and other forms of diagnostic imagery have failed, and attempts at exploratory surgery have triggered its defense mechanisms which are both painful and deadly.

When it perceives that it is being threatened in some way, SCP-203 is capable of emitting a high-frequency droning sound that has a profoundly damaging effect on the human nervous system.

The effects of this defense mechanism were able to be observed directly when a D Class Personnel accidentally struck SCP-203 and its droning sound was activated.

Immediately after being exposed to the sound, D-104 experienced a severe headache.

After 15 minutes the headache grew worse and D-104 began to bleed from the ears.

After a half hour, the D Class, who had now gone to the infirmary, began to experience seizures and was bleeding from all of his orifices.

Ten minutes later, the D Class was dead.

Another test was performed and the results were nearly identical, with symptoms progressing at roughly the same rate.

However this time, rather than move the D Class to the infirmary, it was kept in the cell with SCP-203.

After forty minutes, the D Class was dead, and a few minutes later, 203 finally ceased its droning sound.

SCP-203 then approached the body of the deceased D Class and began to use its own augmentations to start removing the skeleton of the D Class.

While SCP-203 was stopped before it could complete its task, it now appears that the droning sound it produces is a defense mechanism, but may also be a part of the process by which it creates new instances of SCP-203.

In interviews with SCP-203, it claims to have no memories of its life prior to its augmentation. It says that it now exists in a near constant state of pain and confusion and that the times when its battery is expended and it enters a rest state are its only escape from the pain of its existence.

It also claims that it has no memory of what happens once its defense mechanism is activated, nor does it remember what it did to the body of the D Class that was left in its cell.

However it is unknown just how truthful SCP-203 is being.

There has been no way to verify anything that SCP-203 tells researchers, and for the time being, its statements are to be regarded by Foundation staff as an attempt to elicit sympathy or otherwise manipulate them emotionally.

It's made several requests for pain killing medication and anesthetics, but so far all of these requests have been denied.

SCP-203 has been classified as Euclid, and it is kept in a specialized storage bunker at a research site.

Two D Class personnel equipped with sound filtering equipment guard it at all times, and it is accompanied by an armed escort to any testing or research sessions.

Is SCP-203 the ultimate victim?

A normal human that was transformed against his will into a crude amalgamation of man and machine?

Maybe there is something more to SCP-203, or rather less.

Is SCP-203 fooling all of us?

Is this Tortured Iron Soul nothing more than a metallic monster, disguising itself with the skin of its last victim?

Perhaps with more research, we will one day know the answer.

15. SCP-173 NEW REVISED ENTRY

A group of three Class D Personnel approach the locked containment chamber.

One of them is carrying a bucket and mop, but all three of them look jumpy and hesitant to move forward.

An SCP Foundation guard walking behind them gives one of them a push forward with the barrel of his gun and they continue stepping towards the cell door.

All three of them nervously stare at the heavy, locked metal door.

Behind it, the sound of stone scraping against metal can be heard coming from inside.

A second guard standing next to the door asks the three if they are ready.

They don't answer and the guard starts to laugh.

They never are.

The guard loudly announces that "special containment procedures are beginning now!

You know the rules.

Two maintain eye contact at all times while the other cleans.

If you have to blink, do it one eye at a time.

And announce before you close even one eye so everyone knows."

The guard turns and starts to enter a code into the keypad next to the door.

Each of the D Classes take a couple hard, last blinks, taking the last opportunity they have to shut both of their eyes at the same time before they begin.

With a loud hiss the sealed chamber door unseals.

"Alright, eyes up!" the guard commands.

The door opens to reveal a small, dimly lit chamber.

There are no furnishings, and much of the metal floor and walls are covered in a reddish brown substance.

And there in the corner, is what they've heard stories and rumors about.

The thing that has given them nightmares ever since they learned that they would have to enter its containment chamber... SCP-173.

Or as most of the staff in the SCP Foundation call it...

The Sculpture.

It looks so unassuming in person.

Just a crude, concrete figure with a stupid looking spray painted face, standing motionless in the corner.

The three D classes get another push from the guard behind them and they enter the chamber.

The two assigned to watch SCP-173 assume their position in the middle of the room, their eyes locked on the Sculpture as the other starts cleaning the foul substance off the floor and walls.

It smells terrible, like a mix of old blood and human waste.

The two assigned to watch 173 pay no attention to the one cleaning though.

They follow protocol to a tee, maintaining their vigil and announcing each time they are going to blink, even if it is only one eye.

The third one continues cleaning, trying his best to keep his own eyes locked on the sculpture as he attempts to mop around it without getting too close.

D-5933 does his job and doesn't break eye contact with SCP-173.

Even though it hasn't moved, he can feel the presence of the Sculpture, something within it, just waiting for him to slip up, to let his eyes avert for just one split second.

They say that's all it takes.

You stop looking for even an instant and it's all over.

With all of the fear coursing through his veins it is hard to maintain focus.

All he can think about is how dry his eyes feel, and blinking them one at a time never seems to be enough.

He wants so badly to shut his eyes, to end their itchy, dry feeling, but he can't.

Even with another watcher it's too risky.

There's suddenly a loud crack but D-5933 doesn't move his eyes away from 173.

He can see in his periphery that the other D Class dropped his broom and instinctively looked down at it.

Luckily for him, there were others watching.

D-5933 shifts in place, taking a step back and bumps into something.

He can't look at what it is, but he reaches behind him and feels that it's the other D Class watcher.

But wait a minute, why is he facing the other way?

"What are you doing, what's going on?" he asks, his eyes never leaving SCP-173.

"What are you talking about?" the other D Class asks back.

"You're facing the wrong way."

"I'm facing the wrong way?

You're facing the wrong way!"

"We're supposed to be watching 173!

What are you looking at?"

"I AM looking at 173.

What are you looking at?!"

D-5933 doesn't know what's going on and starts to panic.

The one cleaning is focused on his task, trying as hard as he can to quickly mop up an especially dirty corner of the cell.

"Ah ah ah…"

It's the worst sound D-5933 could have heard.

"Ah-choo!"

A sneeze.

Just inches behind his head.

Followed by the sound of bones being cracked, a scream that was cut off too short, and then a sick, thud as a body dropped to the floor.

D-5933 doesn't even have a chance to scream before a pair of concrete hands grab his neck, and his own head is twisted around to see another identical looking sculpture staring back at him.

"Ladies and gentlemen of the O5 council, we have a problem."

A senior researcher is giving a presentation to a group who remain largely in the shadows, obscuring both their identities as well as their reactions to this horrendous news.

"SCP-173, through means which we have not yet been able to determine… has multiplied."

There's no reaction from any of the thirteen figures seated around the large, curved table.

The researcher in charge of SCP-173 waits for a response, anything at all, but after receiving none he clears his throat and continues.

"We gave each of the new instances their own designation, SCP-173-1 and SCP-173-2.

Two of the D-Class on observation duty during the regular cleaning of 173's cell were killed, the third was able to keep them both in his line of sight until they could be re-contained and moved into separate cells."

Again, no reaction from the shadows.

"But as you know… this wasn't the end of it.

At some point, the instances of SCP-173 multiplied again.

Each splitting to form yet another instance.

SCP-173-1 through 4 are all contained separately, but we don't know if or when another split will occur."

The senior researcher waits, but no one on the O5 council speaks or moves, until the one seated in the very middle, slides a piece of paper across the table in front of him.

The senior researcher looks confused, he looks to the Mobile Task Force guard stationed near the door, but he too remains expressionless, eyes locked straight ahead.

The researcher, unsure of what else to do, steps away from the lectern and walks towards the table.

He picks up the piece of paper and reads it:

OBJECT CLASS - UPGRADE FROM EUCLID TO KETER
ORDERS - CONTINUE OBSERVATION

The senior researcher nods in agreement, thanks the O5 Council for their time, and leaves the room.

Lights flash and siren blare in the halls of Site-19.

It's a containment breach.

Facility staff, researchers, and site guards all run down the hall screaming, trying desperately to get away.

There's no hope for any of them though.

In a flash, SCP-173 instances appear behind them, snapping their necks and dropping them to the floor before moving on to their next victim.

There must be dozens of them.

Even as a guard tries to keep their eyes on one instance, preventing it from moving, another appears behind them.

The staff of Site-19 flee for their lives, screaming for someone, anyone, to help them.

The senior researcher presses pause on the video, the terrified face of the senior researcher who gave the last presentation is frozen on the screen.

An instance of SCP-173 is directly behind them, its hands wrapped around his neck in the split second before his life was snuffed out.

The new researcher giving the presentation looks considerably more frazzled than his predecessor.

He explains to the O5 council that following this horrific containment breach at Site-19, at least 61 instances of SCP-173 are now unaccounted for.

It is still unknown how they are replicating, but worryingly there is evidence that the process may be speeding up.

He presses play on a new clip from the security footage which shows what appears to be multiple instances of 173 working in tandem, some using their bodies to block exits, others creating choke points in the facility corridors.

"We have theorized that SCP-173, as we are now referring to the collective instances, may possess a form of hive intelligence.

It also appears that this intelligence scales with the number of instances that are nearby.

This allowed them to implement tactics that thwarted our containment efforts, as they used instances to block our containment teams from being able to pursue others."

"What you have in front of you is a proposal for Revised Special Containment Procedures."

"What I recommend may sound drastic, but it's what I truly believe is the only way to contain this threat."

Each of the O5 Council Members picks up the folder in front of them, bringing it into the shadows that obscure them.

"What I propose is that SCP-173 instances no longer be kept in containment cells, but instead placed inside of form-fitting metal containers.

We can then use SCP-120 to transport the instances to the Foundation site on the lunar surface.

The facility will have to be abandoned of course, it's too risky to maintain a presence there, but each of the instances will be fitted with a tracking collar to ensure that we will be able to detect if any of them are somehow able to escape."

The senior researcher waits.

After a time, a paper is once again slid across the table.

He approaches and picks it up, he sees that it is the same folder containing his Revised Special Containment Procedures proposal.

He opens it to find that it has been stamped "APPROVED".

"BREAKING NEWS" flashes across the screen.

A worried looking reporter appears as though she didn't have time to do her hair or makeup before rushing on air to deliver this special report.

She explains that civilian deaths across North America are now estimated to be more than 500,000 people in the last 48 hours, as these still unidentified creatures continue their deadly rampage across the continent.

It is unknown how many of them there may be, but the number of sightings has led some to estimate that there may be hundreds if not thousands or even tens of thousands of these living, neck snapping sculptures.

The reporter explains that rumors are circulating that the creature can be stopped by maintaining eye contact with it, but that this has yet to be confirmed.

There is still no official word from the White House or from any members of Congress, and their current location and status are unknown following reports that most of Washington D.C. was overrun by the creatures earlier that day.

The reporter suddenly stops speaking and a terrified look comes over her face, her eyes locked on something just off screen.

The camera pans over to show an instance of SCP-173 standing over a dead cameraman.

There's a scream, and the camera goes back to the reporter who now lies dead on her desk, her head twisted 180 degrees, before there's another sound of bones breaking and the feed goes dead.

A woman in an SCP researcher coat sits at a computer terminal in a secure bunker, a large, jeweled medallion around her neck, typing furiously, as if there isn't much time.

"Personal Log of Dr. Bright.

From the little news I've been able to gather, it sounds like SCP-173 has besieged and destroyed four Foundation facilities pretty much simultaneously in the last 24 hours.

Each instance shows the same strength as the original, and thousands of them working together are capable of ripping open concrete bunkers and compromising foot-thick steel doors.

I alone have been killed thirty-seven times in the last week.

They can smell me, somehow, regardless of what body I'm in.

The majority decision of the remaining O5s is that this is an XK class end of the world scenario unfolding, and they're gonna deal with the problem, or else the Russians are.

They're evacuating this base, which means there won't be a single Foundation scientist anywhere in the New World.

They say they're gonna try to evacuate the surviving civilians, but I doubt it.

There can't be more than a couple hundred people in all of North America anyway.

I managed to make it down to a secure bunker but who knows how long it will be until they're able to get in.

I don't think there's any chance I can get out either.

I'm running out of food, and I'm not sure which will get me first, hunger, the sculptures, or what I know the O5's will inevitably do."

Dr. Bright closes the computer terminal and sits back in her chair.

She looks up at the ceiling of the bunker where the sound of concrete scratching against metal can be heard through the thick walls.

A sullen and tired looking researcher steps out of a room in the makeshift foundation site that has been established just outside of Amsterdam in the Netherlands.

He's holding a piece of paper and closes the door behind him which has had "O5 Council

- Authorized Entry Only" hastily painted on the outside.

A small group of Foundation staff are waiting for him, they've gathered to hear what the Overseers have decided to do in the face of this world ending disaster.

The researcher looks around at his colleagues' faces, and as they make eye contact, any hope they had is quickly replaced by the bad news they know is coming.

He begins to read:

"Revised Special Containment Procedures Containment Zone X1, formerly North and South America, is to be denied access.

Following saturation nuclear bombing the number of SCP-173 instances has been reduced.

All available Foundation resources are to be redirected to monitoring the ocean, to ensure the integrity of Containment Zone X1.

Foundation Adjuncts from national navies are to perform around the clock patrols and sonar sweeps.

Detected instances are to be contained and removed to SCP-120 for transport to the lunar containment site."

"That's it?" one of the staff members asks.

"That's it," the researcher replies.

Several of those present begin to cry.

There's nothing more they can do.

Their homes, their friends, their families, all of them are gone.

Killed either by the neck wrenching sculptures or in the heat of a nuclear blast.

"Why, why did they have to do it?" one of the other staff who appears to be a former site guard asks.

"That's all we could do!" another argues.

There's much disagreement in the small crowd.

No matter how they feel though, this was the official order from the O5 Council, their word is law.

Especially in a world where all law and order outside of the Foundation has broken down.

There really was no other option.

All they can do now is hope that the sacrifice of two whole continents was enough to keep it contained.

That SCP-173 is unable to cross the ocean to Europe, and that they remain safe on this side of the planet.

The group grows quiet, mourning the loss of the world they once knew, when the silence is suddenly interrupted by someone running down the hall.

It's another researcher carrying his own piece of paper.

He tries to push past the group towards the O5 Council's door, insisting that they let him through, that he has important news that can't wait.

"What is it?" demands the group, "we deserve to know!"

The group wrestles the paper away from the junior researcher and it is passed through the group to the same man who read the Revised Special Containment Procedures.

He quickly reads the report, it's just a couple of lines, and his face goes white.

"What is it, what does it say?" comes a question from the crowd.

"Message from the North Atlantic Navy General Command.

Verified sighting of SCP-173 in the United Kingdom.

Nuclear bombardment authorized and executed.

No survivors."

SCP-173 has come for them.

16. SCP-4434 –ANGLERFISH

There are no streetlights on this stretch of the old, narrow road, which runs through a rural part of West Virginia. A car has gone off the road into a ditch and needs to be pulled out.

A common task for this tow truck driver and he's often in the area doing similar jobs, though he's never been on this particular road and he has to keep his eyes peeled for any signs or other markers that might give him an idea of how close he is to his turn.

He spots something up ahead, but as he gets closer he sees that it isn't a road sign, it's a billboard. As he passes by he can make out the weathered lettering advertising a diner twenty miles down the road that's probably been closed for at least as many years.

As he continues driving he sees more dilapidated billboards, advertising other long since shuttered businesses like gas stations and autobody shops.

But then he sees one on the road ahead of him that's nothing like the others.

This one doesn't look old at all. In fact it looks quite new. He drives by and has to question if he saw it correctly. It seemed like all it said was "Get Away" over and over and then the name of a road. Is that an invitation? Or a warning? It wasn't even clear what kind of business it might be advertising. He continues driving, but he can't quit thinking about that strange sign. He even feels compelled to turn around so he can get another look at it, but there's no need, because as he rounds a curve there's another of the same sign. This time he slows down as he passes to get a better look and he was right, it just says "Get Away" multiple times with the name of a road. Wagriwa Road. Must be Native American or something.

Now he really can't get the billboard out of his mind. What does it mean?

What is it advertising? And why is there a third one of them just ahead of him?!

He pulls his truck to the side of the road, stopping with his headlights illuminating the sign.

He gets out of the truck and stands in front of the billboard. It's just the same as the others. Get away written over and over. Wagriwa Road. He can see now that the background of the sign is a picture of some trees on a gray, cloudy winter day.

He also notices for the first time that there's another line at the bottom.

Find what you are looking for. What does it mean? Find what you're looking for on Wagriwa Road? Where even is that? There's no directions. No address. No phone number.

He takes a step back from the sign and looks up and down the darkened road. What is he doing out here on the side of the road? Someone is stranded in a ditch waiting for him and he's staring at a billboard? He gets back into the truck, puts it in gear, and drives away.

As he continues down the tree lined rural road though, he inevitably finds his thoughts turning back to the signs.

Get away. But find what you're looking for? It doesn't make any sense. Or are you supposed to get away to Wagriwa Road? Who would put these up? And why do they look so new? Everything else out here looks like it's for a business that shut down years ago? What are they trying to -

He suddenly slams on his brakes and comes to a screeching stop in the middle of the road.

His eyes are locked on what's in front of him. His headlights aren't lighting up another billboard though, this time it is a worn road sign... Wagriwa Road.

He can't help it. He has to know what's down this road.

He has to know what these signs are about. The stuck driver can wait a few minutes longer.

He turns his truck onto the narrow gravel road and drives for a few hundred yards, following it around a couple of bends as it winds through the trees, until it abruptly ends. There's nothing out here, no buildings, no signs, just what looks to be a dirt path leading deeper into the woods.

The tow truck driver switches off the ignition and the road is plunged into darkness.

He reaches under his seat and takes out a flashlight before getting out of the truck.

He shines the light into the woods surrounding him but there's nothing to see... no wait, there is something, and it's coming down the path out of the trees.

"Phil? Phil is that you?" The figure that stepped out of the woods is talking to him.

He shines his flashlight at them and they raise a hand to shade their eyes from the light.

"Sharon?! What are you doing out here?" It's Sharon, the tow truck driver's ex-wife, but he thought she'd moved to Colorado after she remarried, why would she be here?

And what was she doing emerging from the woods?

"Phil, come here. I need to show you something."

He hesitates for just a moment, but then finds that he's walking towards his ex-wife.

Before he can reach her she turns and starts walking down the path back into the woods and he follows. He walks just behind her, his flashlight illuminating the path in front of them.

He thinks he hears a rustling coming from the woods next to him and searches the trees with his flashlight but doesn't see anything.

"Come on, it's just a little further," she says.

"Where are we going? What's just a little further?"

"What you are looking for."

The woods suddenly open up and he finds that they are standing in a clearing. She stops walking and he pauses next to her. He opens his mouth to speak but she quickly shushes him.

"Quiet, they're almost here."

The tow truck driver looks around but he doesn't see anything, just the faint outline of trees that are barely visible on this moonless night. But then he watches as several creatures begin to emerge out of the woods into the clearing. They're… deer?

He watches as just a few come towards him at first, but then he notices that they have completely surrounded him. There must be over twenty.

"Turn off your light" she tells him.

He obeys and in the darkness he can see now that there is something special about these deer. Their eyes are glowing with a pale white light. One of the smaller deer steps forward and cautiously approaches him. He squats down and holds his hand out, showing it that he means it no harm.

The deer looks back nervously at a larger one that he thinks must be its mother.

It looks like it nods in approval, and the smaller deer moves closer.

He can clearly see its big, beautiful doe eyes glow brightly in the dark.

"You're okay" he says, and leans forward to give it a reassuring pet when -

Following the mysterious disappearances of multiple people in an area of West Virginia near the town of Harpers Ferry, the SCP Foundation soon became interested in a particular stretch of road where it appeared that many of those who had gone missing had traveled just prior to their vanishing.

Agents were dispatched to the area and immediately detected high levels of thaumaturgic energy, with the epicenter appearing to be on a plot of privately owned land. Investigation of local records revealed that the land was owned by a man named Richard Redkinne. The Foundation staff contacted Mr. Redkinne under the guise of being federal agents investigating a crime that had been committed on the property while he was away. Mr. Redkinne happily cooperated with the agents, explaining to them that had never experienced any abnormal events on the property while he was living there, but that he had not resided on the land for some time. Strangely he claimed to not know the road as Wagriwa Road, insisting that as far as he knew it had never had an official name, being nothing more than a long driveway out to his property. When asked if he could remember anything else abnormal about the location, he told the agents no, but that his daughter had written many fictional stories about strange happenings on the land, and perhaps those had somehow turned into rumors and then urban legends, though that was a long time ago. When the agents requested to meet with the daughter he explained that it was impossible, she had drowned many years prior in the nearby Shenandoah River.

The agents again examined the local records and found that Mr. Redkinne wasn't lying, his daughter really had passed away and her body was found in the river.

The timing of this accident was quite coincidental though, as it had occurred exactly one week before the first missing person in the area was reported.

Quickly realizing that something was not quite right with this piece of land,

the SCP Foundation authorized the purchase from Mr. Redknine, who was more than happy to sell, and a research outpost was constructed to further investigate the anomalous events which had collectively been dubbed SCP-4434. While exploring the surrounding area, they soon found what so many others had before - the bizarre billboards imploring one to both "get away" as well as come to Wagriwa Road to "find what you are looking for."

The signs, which were designated as SCP-4434-A, were found on roads across the West Virgina, Maryland, Virginia tri-state area, but their locations would often change, with the billboards only manifesting for short amounts of time before vanishing and reappearing elsewhere. Bizarrely, when attempts were made to photograph or videotape the signs, the resulting footage would show only a blank, white sign.

The Foundation knew that they needed to investigate further, and several experiments were authorized to find just what was happening on the land at the end of the mysterious road.

A D-Class personnel, D-84021, was given a radio and implanted with GPS locators in his neck, torso, and thigh, and sent down the road with orders to report back on what they experienced, though unlike the people who had gone missing, he was not shown the billboard prior to entering the area.

The D-Class walked to the end of the road where he reported that a creature was emerging from a path leading into the woods. He soon exclaimed that the creature was a dog that he used to own. The researchers monitoring the test were confused, since the dog had apparently been deceased for some time, and yet here it was standing in front of him. Although the D-Class had seemed hesitant at the start of the mission, once he saw his childhood dog, all of his fears were set aside and he willingly followed it deeper into the forest.

After 90 seconds, the D-Class reported that he had entered a clearing and was being surrounded by a group of deer. The reports stopped soon after and were replaced by the sound of screams as D-84021 was attacked and apparently consumed by the deer. Two of the three GPS trackers remained active for the next forty minutes, and SCP researchers followed their path as they moved to the middle of the clearing and then appeared to enter into a sinkhole or cave of some sort,

where they traveled slowly in a winding pattern downward until contact was lost.

Following this test, the Foundation researchers suspected that the creature that would emerge from the woods, which had been designated as SCP-4434-B, was able to change forms into one that would be trusted by those who entered the 4434 area.

The deer, on the other hand, seemed to always maintain their appearance, and the whole group was designated as SCP-4434-C. The tests were far from over though.

For the next, two D-Classes were sent into SCP-4434 in order to see what form 4434-B would take when more than one person was present. Just like before, an entity emerged from the woods, but this time it took the form of a young man in a suit who immediately offered to clear any and all debts the D-Classes held as well as expunging their criminal records, freeing them from their life as test subjects. All they would need to do is follow him into the woods.

The agents monitoring the test ordered the D-Classes not to follow the man, but they were ignored, and the researchers listened as they instead began conversing with SCP-4434-B, seeming to be quite interested in his offer. They soon followed him into the woods, and just over two minutes later, they too were attacked and consumed by SCP-4434-C.

It appeared now that once someone entered the SCP-4434 area, they were all but helpless to resist the compulsive effects of SCP-4434-B.

The Foundation researchers wanted to test the limits of SCP-4434's power, and so they then came up with a rather creative procedure for the next test.

Another D-Class personnel was sent down the road, but this one was wearing a body harness that was connected to a pulley system, as well as being equipped with a camera.

He was ordered to wait at the edge of the SCP-4434 area until the 4434-B entity appeared.

The entity soon emerged, taking the form of a middle aged woman. As soon as the D Class was seen conversing with the entity and agreed to follow it, the pulley was engaged in order to forcibly pull him out of the area. This was followed by an entirely unexpected event. The middle aged woman quickly produced a knife, and with a supernatural speed, severed the rope on the pulley system.

The now freed D-Class stood up, followed the woman into the woods, and was consumed soon after.

The researchers were growing frustrated with their lack of advancement in understanding the anomaly, and so for the fourth test, they decided to take quite extreme measures. A drone was used to fly over the area, which identified the mouth of the cave that the GPS trackers had been taken into.

It was a three and a half meter wide hole in the ground, too dark to see anything past the entrance, and the drone installed an anchor point in the ground at the mouth of the hole before flying in to explore further, but the signal was almost immediately lost. Progress had been made though.

Yet another D-Class was selected, this time one who had climbing experience.

D-84041 was warned in advance that the SCP-4434-B entity would appear to her and would have a compulsive affect, and that she was to ignore them no matter what form they took and instead proceed as quickly as possible to the cave, which had been designated as SCP-4434-D.

D-84041 was taken to the road, and she immediately began running down the path into the woods. She was able to reach the mouth of the cave without seeing any anomalous entities, neither 4434-B nor the carnivorous deer. She quickly attached the rope she had brought to the anchor that was installed by the drone and began rappelling into the hole.

As she descended down, she described a normal, rocky cave, one that grew wetter the further down she went. Surprisingly, she soon reached the bottom, where she found a spherical room, roughly eight meters across, but this was not anything like the entrance to the cave. The floor of this room wasn't made of rock or dirt, it was more like flesh, and it appeared... to be breathing. And there was something else down there too, a folded piece of paper with writing on it.

The D-Class was ordered to pick up the paper, take a sample of the cave floor, and exit the area as soon as possible, as there was no way to predict if the SCP-4434-B and C entities, or something worse, would soon appear. After taking a sample she began climbing out of the cave. When she emerged there were still no signs of any anomalous creatures but she quickly made her way down the road and out of the SCP-4434 area.

When she reached the waiting Agents at the edge of the area, D-84041 handed them the sample and the paper that she found but then stopped and turned around. There on the ground roughly five meters away was a plate of food. Without any hesitation she walked back into the SCP-4434 area, picked up the plate, and walked back into the woods. She was never seen again.

It was now clear that 4434-B could take forms other than just humanoids and animals.

As the objects that the D-Class had managed to get out of SCP-4434 were analyzed, the area's former owner, Richard Redkinne, was again questioned by Foundation agents.

They asked him if there was anything that he failed to mention in their previous interview and he told them that there was one thing that he preferred not to normally discuss.

Just before his daughter's death, in addition to her fascination with writing and coming up with stories, she had become obsessed with the occult. When they asked him about the paper they had found within SCP-4434-D, he told them that it was very likely that she had written it.

The SCP Foundation now understood why they had detected so many thaumaturgic particles in the area, which is the residual energy left over from a particular form of ritualistic practice that is more commonly known as "magic" or "witchcraft."

The contents of the paper found in the cave seem to add additional weight to the theory that his daughter may have been involved in a ritual that led to the creation of SCP-4434, because written on the single page is a poem which reads:

The forest is a sea; the wind is the waves and the water is the leaves. The streams become undercurrents, the birds become fish,and coral finds its home as fungus, growths sprouting as I wish.

The ground is the shore, pulling me by the feet,dragging me down and pulling me back Back and forth on repeat.

I dove down past the light down where I couldn't breathe, and found nature looking for a fight.

Yes, the forest is a sea, but I've made it barely big enough for me.

The forest is a sea, so now something's bound to come eat.

Things only became more mysterious though when Foundation researchers performed a DNA test on the sample taken from the bottom of the SCP-4434-D cave. What they found was that it was, just as D-84041 had described, a flesh-like substance. And that it was a 78.9% match to Melanocetus johnsoni, better known as the Deep Sea Anglerfish.

And there was one final discovery to be made as well. Linguistic teams within the Foundation investigated the name of the road that had appeared on the SCP-4434-A billboards and discovered that the word was very similar to the Native American Tutelo tribe word wágriwa, which roughly translates to the phrase... I have come back.

17. SCP-799 CARNIVOROUS BLANKET

A storm rages outside of the little old house, as inside, a little old woman bounces a little baby on her little old knee.

The baby coos and laughs as the old woman makes funny faces and noises for the child, trying to keep it entertained as they wait for his parents to return from their much needed night out by themselves.

The old woman herself needs a rest now though, she's forgotten how exhausting it can be to watch a child.

"Okay, that's enough.

It's time for both of us to take a little nap before your parents get back."

She gets up and takes the baby into a nearby room that looks as though it was a nursery at one time, but it hasn't been used for many years.

As she goes to set the child into the crib, a strong gust of wind blows through the room.

She places the baby down and rushes to the window and closes it shut.

It must have been left cracked open by mistake.

Brrr.

The room is cold from the wind, but she has just the thing to fix that.

She moves to a small closet and opens the creaky door.

The little old woman strains to reach up to the top shelf and feels around.

Ah, there it is!

She pulls down a baby blanket, a soft baby blue with colorful animals printed on it.

It looks as though it's been up there for a long time and she gives it a good shake before walking back to the crib.

"Look what we have here!

It's your daddy's own blankie!"

She gives it another shake.

"There we go, good as new."

She leans into the crib and wraps the small, helpless child in the blanket before giving him a gentle kiss on the forehead.

"Now you get some sleep.

Your mommy and daddy will be back before you know it and we want to show them what a good babysitter grammie, don't we?

That way I get to see you all the time."

The little old woman switches off the light and exits the room, leaving the door cracked just a few inches.

She heads back to the couch and plops down on it.

Almost as soon as she does though, the baby starts crying.

With a sigh she gets back up and goes back to the nursery.

"What's the matter, little dear?" she says as she turns the lights on.

"Oh no!" she rushes to the crib, "you've kicked your blanket off! You must be freezing."

She grabs the blanket from the end of the crib and tucks it around the baby once again.

"There you go, that's better."

The old woman leaves the room and quietly closes the door shut, leaving it open just a few inches.

The moment she turns around to go back to the couch though, the crying starts again.

With a sigh she opens the door and goes back into the room.

Once again, the blanket is stuffed at the end of the crib where the baby has kicked it off.

"Fine.

Don't want a blanket?

That's fine."

She picks the baby up out of the crib and rocks him in her arms until it stops crying.

She sets him back in the crib.

"There you go.

No blankets.

Just please, get some sleep.

Grammie's tired."

The old woman takes the blanket out of the crib and leaves the room.

She closes the door most of the way and, incredibly, this time the child remains silent.

The old woman resumes her place on the couch and starts to yawn.

Just as she does, the wind outside picks up and howls loudly.

The old woman shivers.

She looks next to her and spots the baby blanket.

She picks it up and examines the cute animal print, remembering when her own son was a baby wrapped in it.

She smiles at the happy thought and throws the blanket around her shoulders.

She leans back on the couch and finds that her eyes are growing very heavy.

She'll rest them for just a moment. She won't fall asleep.

She'll just… rest.

"Mom?

It's us, we're back.

Thanks again for - " The couple both scream when they enter the house to find that the old woman is lying facedown on the floor in a pool of blood.

The source of the blood is obvious, chunks of flesh from her shoulders and upper back have been torn out, leaving jagged holes, as if she were mauled by an animal.

As the man runs to the old woman, trying to do anything he can to help her, the woman runs to the nursery to find…

That the baby is sleeping peacefully in his crib.

The woman picks up the child, tears streaming down her cheeks, and returns to the living room to see her husband kneeling beside his dead mother.

Both the husband and wife are so shocked by what they have found that neither notices the baby blanket lying on the couch, or that the cruel, blood covered mouth on it is slowly fading from view until it disappears completely.

There is little in life that is more comforting than a favorite blanket.

Perhaps you've had the same one since you were a child, or you have a heavy one that you like to wrap yourself in when you're feeling down, or maybe it's just one that's especially fluffy and warm that you'd do anything to keep.

Today's anomaly plays on those very feelings, using them against its victims to become one of the more insidious predatory anomalies in the SCP Foundation archives.

This is SCP-799, also known as… the Carnivorous Blanket.

SCP-799 is a type of creature that can vary in shape, size, and appearance, but, as the name implies, always takes the form of a blanket of some kind.

The exact material the anomaly is made out of is unknown, but it is a very soft fiber that in many ways resembles a high-quality merino wool blend, though one that retains heat even more effectively than its natural counterpart.

SCP-799's weight can vary from between half a kilogram all the way to six kilograms, and while examples have been found in nearly every color imaginable, it seems predisposed towards pastels, and will frequently have patterns featuring stylized, friendly depictions of various animals.

Both the pastel colors and the childish patterns are especially common in instances of SCP-799 that weigh less than two kilograms and would colloquially be known as "baby blankets."

While SCP-799 is undoubtedly a living organism, there is some debate as to whether it is itself an animal, or perhaps a type of fungal colony.

Instances of 799 are incapable of locomotion, lying motionless for long periods of time, and require little in the way of nutrition.

What small amount they do need, they appear to be able to gain almost entirely from the organic particles present in normal household dust, such as animal dander and dead human skin cells.

The blanket feeds via a series of minute, filter feeding mouth-like structures that are spread across the surface of the creature, which wait for nutrients to fall into them, not unlike a sponge on the ocean floor.

Instances of SCP-799 can survive for quite a while in this state, and one specimen was noted as having lived for multiple years in a damp attic, subsisting entirely on the small organic particles that would drift down from the rafters above.

Should an instance of SCP-799 be forced to go for long periods of time without a source of nutrition though, like when, for example, it is placed inside of a sealed closet or drawer, it will begin to undergo certain physical changes, which result in it metamorphosing into its predatory form.

These changes aren't noticeable from only casual observation, and consist of the blanket converting its many filter feeding mouths into a single, large one, that is lined with multiple rows of extremely sharp teeth.

The blanket creature also develops a new form of tissue inside its cloth-like structure, one that is similar to muscle and capable of contracting and squeezing.

Once its metamorphosis is complete, the instance of SCP-799 will lie in wait for an unsuspecting creature to cover themselves with it or wrap it around their body.

Once they do, the blanket will bide its time until they enter a state of rest, usually

waiting for them to fall asleep entirely, at which point, it's feeding phase will begin.

Once the creature has detected that its victim is dormant, it will use its newly formed muscle to latch onto them, holding them in place as it opens its tooth-lined maw.

It will begin to bite at its confined prey, tearing off several kilograms of flesh, bone, and any other organic material it can, swallowing it, and converting it into a thin slurry that it spreads through its body almost immediately.

This traumatic, violent process nearly always leads to the victim dying of blood loss.

Within ten minutes of the attack, the mouth on SCP-799 will have been completely reabsorbed, leaving no signs that it is anything other than a normal, everyday blanket, though one which now mysteriously weighs several kilograms more than it did before.

By forty minutes after the attack, the entire digestive system within SCP-799 will have de-metamorphosed back into its original form, with the single digestive tract being changed once again to the many dispersed filter feeding mouths.

While SCP-799 is more than happy to feed on any warm blooded animal, including humans, it shows no interest in coldblooded ones or inanimate objects.

It appears then that its senses may be limited to only touch and heat, using those as signs that it is now wrapped around a potential meal.

Adding to the strangeness of SCP-799 is that it reproduces through "budding," like flatworms and corals.

When it has absorbed enough nutrients and sufficiently increased its mass, either very slowly through filter feeding or rapidly via its carnivorous phase, it will begin to take on a quilt-like appearance.

Over several weeks, one of the quilt squares will puff up and slide off the blanket.

This new, smaller instance will resemble a doily or throw pillow, until it too begins to feed and grow.

The new instance is a perfect clone of its parent, identical in every way, and it will eventually grow to a similar size and begin its own reproductive cycle.

It is unknown exactly how long it takes SCP-799 to reach full maturity, but the current best guess is that when kept in its filter feeding phase, an instance will reproduce every fifty to sixty years.

Instances of SCP-799 are quite prevalent across the planet, and the SCP Foundation currently has hundreds of examples in containment.

Unfortunately, it is unknown just how many still exist in the wild, as it is very difficult to identify instances with one of the only reliable means being through genetic testing.

Should any instances be located though, they are to be destroyed immediately, as the Foundation already has a large enough population in containment for research purposes, and they pose too much of a risk both in terms of harm and exposure to the general public.

SCP-799 has been classified as Euclid, and each instance is kept in its own, separate, bio-containment cell at Bio-Site-66.

Dust is regularly collected from the on site, D-Class personnel dorms and is sprinkled over the blankets regularly to keep them in their filter feeding state, though only just enough to hopefully maintain their size and not allow them to reproduce.

Should any small, cloth objects appear in their containment lockers, it is to be removed immediately and contained separately.

SCP-799 isn't the only predatory creature that resembles a cloth good in Foundation containment, and research into possible connections to SCP-1626, the oversized gray hooded sweatshirt that sends penetrating fibers into anyone unlucky enough to put it on, is ongoing.

18. TEOTIHUACAN
PTERODACTYLACTERY- SCP 4959

The explorer slashes his way through the jungle, using his large machete to hack through the thick undergrowth. He suddenly stops and turns around, "Which way was it again?"

His local guide answers but he must wait for him to finish and his research assistant to translate. "He says to continue straight, it's just another hundred yards or so."

The gentleman explorer offers a quick nod before turning to resume cutting his way through the forest. The guide was right though, because after a short way the dense jungle suddenly opens up, giving way to a clearing that reveals one of the most incredible things the explorer has ever seen. Just ahead of him, rising out of the forest is a massive, ancient stone temple. A huge step pyramid of solid stone, intricately carved and covered with elaborate statues.

The colossal structure looks like it has been abandoned for centuries if not longer, with nature having done its best to reclaim the stone and cover the pyramid in vines and other plants.

The team approaches the temple but stops in front of a stone monument that stands in front of it.

The explorer traces its carved lines with his finger, knocking the dirt away to reveal its weathered pictograph. It appears to depict a sort of creature, but with large, spread wings instead of arms. "Perhaps a kind of... ritualistic garb?" the explorer says to his assistant.

The assistant hastily scribbles in her notebook, trying to document everything she can. "Yes, this is definitely a priest-like figure of some kind, maybe a leader of this temple thanks to the connection he shares to their - " the explorer's musings are interrupted by his guide, who he angrily spins around to face.

"Yes, what?! What is it?"

His research assistant translates for him as usual, "he says that we should go no further, that it's too dangerous."

"Nonsense," replies the explorer, "we came all this way, and who knows what fantastic treasures await us inside... Historical treasures I mean, artifacts. Treasures of knowledge, of course."

"Of course," replies his assistant before following her boss as he starts making his way up the step pyramid, as the guide holds true to his stated intentions and waits near the edge of the jungle.

The two of them walk through an entrance that leads into a long, dark hallway. With only torches to light their way, it's impossible to see just how deep it runs into the temple.

The explorer stops to examine the walls which are covered in even more carvings. He can see that there are complicated geometric patterns, but also many more depictions of the same winged creature that was on the monument outside. Here though, the creatures are depicted in moments of action.

They appear to be running, chasing, reaching out and grabbing for... people. They are shown attacking them, picking them up, carrying them away to... right where the pictograph story should reveal its climax is a chunk of missing wall. It must have fallen off at some point.

"Ah, oh well," the explorer declares before moving on to explore more of the temple.

His assistant doesn't follow though. She spots several pieces of stone on the floor underneath the missing panel and kneels down to get a closer look. She begins to gather them together, rearranging the various pieces back into their original form.

Meanwhile the explorer's attention has been caught by something else. On the other side of the hall is a statue of a tall, proud warrior, and in his hand, he clutches a large, bejeweled spear, the gemstones adorning it sparkling in the torchlight.

The explorer reaches out and grips the spear's handle. He begins to pull, perhaps being a little rougher than one should with an ancient artifact, but he wants this fabulous jeweled piece, and even more than the spear itself, he wants the acclaim it will bring him back home.

As the explorer pulls on the spear his research assistant moves the final piece of the broken wall carving into position. She holds her torch over it to get a better look and she gasps.

The winged creatures are carrying people away, but that isn't the end of the story.

They are bringing them somewhere, and she can see now that they are being presented to an even bigger winged creature. It's a monster, a monster that is feeding on the people.

The assistant turns to tell the explorer what she has found, and just as she does, she watches as he is finally able to rend the spear loose from the statue's grip.

The statue finally letting go causes him to fall backwards to the ground where he lies, marveling at the beautiful jeweled spear in his hands.

"Look out!" yells his assistant. The explorer doesn't notice that the statue is precariously rocking back and forth, and he rolls out of the way just before it crashes down right where he was lying and admiring the spear.

"Are you ok?" she asks as she rushes over.

"I think so," he tells her. "Just a little bump on the head. Nothing that can't be fixed up by a good - "

"By a good what?" she asks, but he seems distracted by something behind her.

"By a good… by a good… By god what is that?"

He points and the research assistant turns to see something emerging from a hole in the wall where the statue once stood. It's one of the creatures from the wall carvings. A bizarre half man, half lizard, with wings instead of arms, though there's no flesh at all, the creature is completely made of bone. The two of them both scream at the skeletonized, half-human, and the creature screams right back at them, emitting a shrill, high-pitched squeal.

Suddenly more of the creatures begin to emerge from the hole in the wall, with others crawling out of previously unseen and unnoticed holes in the walls and ceiling.

The creatures rush towards them, blocking their way out of the temple, and the pair have no choice but to run further down the darkened hallway.

As they run, more of the creatures emerge from holes in the darkness, screaming at them and grasping at them with the sharp claws on the end of their wings.

As they round a corner, one reaches out and grasps the explorer's ankle causing him to trip and fall hard onto the stone floor. His assistant rushes to his aid,

but as she is helping him up, two more of the creatures appear behind her and envelop her in their bony, winged arms. The explorer stands up and stabs at one of them with the jeweled spear as they drag her into a dark hole, but a third tears it from his hands.

With more still coming down the hallway behind him, the explorer has to run. The hallway in front of him looks to have collapsed at some point in the past and he has no choice but to enter one of the dark tunnels that has been carved into the rock.

The narrow tunnel winds back and forth and the explorer is unsure of where he is going or what his plan is. He rounds a bend and the tunnel opens up into a gigantic room. The ceiling must be over a hundred feet high, and he can't see the furthest walls with the only light emitted by his torch, and a dim beam of sunlight coming down through a hole high up on the ceiling.

He notices too that it has suddenly gone quiet. He turns and looks back at the tunnel he has just emerged from and notices that the sound of the horrible creatures that were chasing him has ceased. The explorer hears something coming from deeper in the giant room and turns back, peering into the darkness.

There in the single beam of light he sees one of the winged creatures, but it is moving strangely, as if it isn't walking, but floating up into the air. And that's because it isn't walking.

As it gets closer, the explorer can see that the winged creature is stuck on the tooth of a gigantic, monstrous mouth. The huge, winged creature emerges from the darkness into the beam of light, tossing back its giant head to consume the creature that was stuck in its teeth, its bones loudly cracking in its mouth. Now in the light, the explorer can see that the monster, which itself must be hundreds of feet long, is a huge flying lizard of some kind. Or at least it was at one time, since now the majority of its body is made only of bone. What scraps of flesh are left hang off in rotten ribbons. The monster opens its mouth and roars at the explorer, its foul breath smells like a mausoleum opening up hitting the explorer in the face.

The explorer tries to run but the monster swipes out with a bony wing that still has a few blackened strips of leathery skin on it and knocks him to the ground. He is pinned to the floor with a huge spiny claw, as the creature opens its mouth, roaring again before moving its head down to start feasting on its meal.

The explorer closes his eyes, bracing himself to be eaten alive when the creature suddenly lets out an ear piercing scream. The explorer opens his eyes to see the jeweled spear sticking out of one of the few spots of flesh remaining on the creature's clawed foot, and gripping the shaft, is his assistant.

She looks a little worse for wear, but she's alive. She offers him a hand to help him up. They need to get out of there, but first the explorer pulls the spear from the monster's claw. The two start running, doing everything they can to avoid the monster as it claws and swipes at them.

They spot an illuminated opening at the other end of the vast room and with no other option, start heading towards it. As they get closer they can see it's just what they needed - daylight. Escape.

They both slide to a stop at the cusp of the opening, nearly tumbling over the edge. On the other side, the tunnel opening up out of the side of the temple gives way to nothing but air, and a drop of hundreds of feet down to the jungle below. They turn to see the monster still rushing towards them and without time to think any longer they both jump, just seconds before the creature snaps its bony jaws in the place where they were standing.

It's too big to fit anything more than its mouth out the door and it howls and screams as they fall through the air before crashing into the ground below.

The assistant slowly opens her eyes to see someone… It's their guide. He is cradling her head, and asking if she's okay. She sits up, dazed and more than a little bruised from her fall.

She asks the guide where the explorer is, if he's alright, and the guide lowers his eyes, looking as though he'd rather not answer. He points next to them without looking and the assistant turns to see the explorer lying on the ground a few feet away from them, his body impaled on the jeweled spear. History is full of tales and legends about gods, monsters, and everything in between. But not all of these are just stories, and in fact sometimes the reality is even more terrifying than what we could envision. And that is exactly the case when it comes to SCP-4959, also known as the Teotihuacan Pterodactylactery.

SCP-4959 is a huge creature that resembles a pterosaur, which were flying reptiles that existed during the Mesozoic Era. While pterosaurs have been extinct for millions of years, SCP-4959 is very much alive, or at the very least, animate. This massive anomaly, whose wingspan stretches approximately 50 meters, is in a living state of decomposition, with roughly 70% of its flesh having rotted or otherwise fallen away, leaving only small patches of skin and decaying tissue clinging to its bones. The flesh that does remain shows no signs of further decomposition though, as if it is permanently locked into this specific stage of advanced decay.

Tests of 4959's flesh have shown no apparent abnormalities, save for a slightly higher than expected concentration of iridium. Its eyes are no longer present, but the eye sockets somehow shine with a bright green light, though the source of this luminescence is unknown. When angered, the creature also emits a multicolored corona of fire from its wings, skull, and neck.

SCP-4959 was discovered in a gigantic chamber beneath the Temple of the Feathered Serpent in Teotihuacan, Mexico.

A number of tunnels connect to the chamber, and these too are anything but empty.

Lurking within the temple's many twisting passages, are entities that have been designated SCP-4959-A. These are humanoid size creatures appear to be constructed of various human and pterosaur bones, creating an all-new creature that is an amalgamation of both. The bones are connected to a central, stone-like heart, but it is unknown if this heart was carved from stone or if it was at one time a real heart that turned to stone through a process of ossification, nor is it fully understood just how the bones are connected to it or stay together.

The 4959-A entities also have a number of varying adornments on their bodies which can include strips of decayed fabric, feathers, and precious stones, that resemble those worn by the indigenous people who resided in the area many centuries ago.

SCP-4959 is carnivorous, though it is unknown if it requires or simply desires to feed.

Regardless, it seems to be the task of the SCP-4959-A entities to bring it meals, since the 4959 creature itself is too large to leave its chamber beneath the temple.

The hallways and passages that originally connected the temple to the chamber housing SCP-4959 have all collapsed, and the only tunnels now leading to it were most likely dug into the rock and earth by the 4959-A entities. They search through these tunnels, most often working at night, looking for small animals like birds and lizards, but also occasionally finding a larger animal or even a human who has somehow found themselves inside. They will then bring their live prey directly to the giant pterosaur, offering them up as both a meal and a sacrifice. SCP-4959 will then proceed to eat the prey whole, sometimes consuming the 4959-A entity at the same time as well.

The temple itself is covered in carvings and murals that give numerous hints as to the origin of SCP-4959. While it is unknown just how it got there, It appears as though the local people discovered the creature within its chamber, and regarded it as an avatar of their Feathered Serpent god or perhaps another unknown deity. A temple was constructed at the site, and they soon began making sacrifices to the god-creature that lived beneath, starting with small animals, but then progressing to human sacrifices on important holy days.

There is also something else shown in the murals that looks to be of great importance.

It seems as though SCP-4959 possessed a sort of "heart" which is depicted as a large gemstone, described as being "red as blood and bright as the rising sun." This gemstone was previously housed at the pinnacle of the temple, though its current location is unknown.

Following intense study of the site by SCP Foundation historians, a narrative was pieced together that may explain at least some of what happened there.

It seems as though there was an uprising within the local population in roughly the sixth century AD. A conflict had arisen amongst the people as to whether this really was a god, or something else, something evil. Those who doubted the deific origins of SCP-4959 wrested control of the temple and journeyed into its depths to attempt to kill the creature.

The many scorch marks on the wall are a testament to the battle that likely took place, and while they suffered many losses, it appears as though they were at least able to seal the chamber shut.

It is currently unknown what became of the great jewel on top of the temple after this, but its location is of great interest to the Foundation given that it may well be the source of SCP-4959's longevity.

SCP-4959 has been classified as Euclid, and it continues to be contained within the chamber beneath the Temple of the Feathered Serpent, though all of the tunnel entrances leading into it have been blocked by reinforced gates. If new ones are discovered as the result of SCP-4959-A's continued tunneling, they too are to be gated and sealed. Once per week, a large, live animal, most often a cow, is deposited down a shaft that leads directly to the chamber, and so far, this seems to be keeping SCP-4959 content to stay within its tomb.

Just what is SCP-4959? And what are the half-man, half-pterosaur creatures who serve it?

Are they former human sacrifices, now destined to live an eternity in servitude to their master?

If SCP-4959 was a god at one point, the fact that we are now the ones responsible for feeding it and keeping it happy means that in a sense, we're the ones serving it now.

19. SCP-153 DRAIN WORMS

A young man and his girlfriend enter the apartment they share.
She tosses her keys on the entryway table as the man checks the time on his phone, he reminds the young woman that they will need to leave soon if they don't want to miss the movie they have purchased tickets for.
The woman agrees, but she wants to take a quick shower before they leave.
As she goes to freshen up, the man sits down at his computer to get in a quick round or two of his favorite online squad-based first-person shooter.
He puts on his headset and jumps into a game.
Before he knows it, he's just finished his third round.
He checks the time on his phone again and realizes that they are running late.
He takes off his headphones and is confused when he hears what sounds like the shower still running.
He gets up and goes to the bathroom door and listens, the shower is definitely still on.
The man knocks on the door and asks if everything is alright.
He waits a moment but there's no response.
He knocks again and still nothing.
She doesn't usually take showers this long and he immediately worries that she might have passed out or… well he doesn't even want to think about it.
"I'm coming in, okay?" he announces as he opens the door to check on her.
The man immediately notices how steamy the room is, the hot water must have been running for a while and he's worried she really did pass out from the heat.
"What's going on, are you okay?" he asks and when there's no response again he pulls open the shower curtain to find… nothing.
Just an empty tub.
There's no sign of his girlfriend anywhere.
The man is beyond confused.
He turns off the water and goes to the bedroom but she isn't in there either.
He runs to the front door but it's still locked, and her keys are sitting on the table.
He unlocks the door and sticks his head out into the hallway anyway, but nothing is out there.

What is going on?!

He checks the bedroom again, then the bathroom, but she hasn't suddenly reappeared in either.

He's in complete shock, unsure of what could be happening.

He sits down on the toilet and puts his head in his hands, his head is spinning as it feels like the world is suddenly falling down all around him.

The police are immediately suspicious of the man's story.

His girlfriend simply vanished while taking a shower?

"You expect us to believe that?" the detective asks.

The man has no answer though.

It's as if she simply blinked out of existence.

He's convinced she must still be in the building somewhere, that she somehow slipped out without him noticing, but none of the security footage from inside of the building shows anything abnormal.

There's footage from the cameras in the lobby of them entering the building, but nothing after that of her leaving.

Just as in every missing person case like this, the boyfriend is the number one suspect, but without any evidence, they can't hold him any longer.

After many long hours of interviews, they finally allow him to leave, but not back to the apartment since it's an active crime scene.

The man has no family to speak of and his few friends seem to have the same suspicions as the police and want nothing to do with him.

His girlfriend was the only person he truly had in the world and now she's gone.

He's put up in a shabby motel and days pass, then weeks, then months.

But no evidence of the missing woman ever turns up.

The man replays the memory of that day over and over in his head searching for some kind of answer, but try as he might he can't remember anything helpful, no clue as to what could have happened.

The case is completely cold, and has been from the very start.

The police eventually have to move on to newer, more solvable cases, and they finally allow the man to return home.

He's overwhelmed with emotion the first time he enters the apartment.

The place is a mess, it looks like the police turned it inside out looking for clues.

Not knowing what else to do, he starts the long process of cleaning up the apartment.

After hours of putting things away, he eventually gathers the strength to go to the one room he's been avoiding… the bathroom.

He opens the door to the last place he's certain his girlfriend was.

He enters to find that it looks like the rest of the apartment, as if someone has looked at every single object.

But just like him, the police never found any trace of where she went.

After straightening up this last room, he decides that he should take a shower and go to bed.

It fills him with dread to think about standing in the last place he knows where she was, but he's had months to grieve the loss of his girlfriend and he's decided that he needs to move on, whatever that means when someone goes missing without a trace.

He turns on the shower and lets the water heat up before stepping in.

Once he's in, every thought he has is about her.

He wonders if she ever actually got in the shower at all, or somehow used it as a diversion to slip out unseen.

He just can't figure out how.

The day's events race through his mind, just as they have a thousand times before, but his thoughts are interrupted when he notices that the water has started to pool around his feet.

He looks down and sees that the drain cover looks normal.

Maybe there's a clog though.

Do showers clog when they're not used?

He has no idea.

He bends down to get a closer look.

The long, black creature emerges from the drain in the blink of an eye and latches onto his mouth, muffling him before he even has a chance to scream.

He struggles and pulls down the curtain on top of him as he falls back onto the shower floor, but it's already too late, and in a matter of minutes, he too will be gone without a trace.

Is there anything more comforting after a hard day than a nice, long, hot shower?

The answer to that is… no.

There is nothing better.

But that relaxing shower might just be the last you ever take when, unbeknownst to you, your pipes are home to an instance of SCP-153, also known as… Drain Worms.

SCP-153 refers to a species that resembles the common nematode or roundworm, consisting of a long, thin body with a large mouth on one end.

While some roundworms can grow to as large as a meter long, which is in itself a disturbing thought, SCP-153 instances can be much, much larger, and it is estimated that they can reach up to nearly 10 meters in length, though it is hypothesized that some instances in the wild may grow even longer.

These worm-like creatures will feed off of any available organic material, however their favorite form of sustenance is fresh animal tissue, and they appear to have an especially strong predilection towards human flesh.

In order to satiate their desire to feed on their preferred prey, SCP-153 has developed a rather unique predatory style that perfectly suits its elongated body structure.

While it is unknown just where they originate, they are most often found in the pipes of sewer and drainage systems.

153 instances will swim up these pipes, seeking out ones that lead to people's homes, and especially those that connect to showers and bathtubs.

Once they reach the end of the pipe, SCP-153 will latch onto the drain cover and begin secreting an acidic substance.

The acid quickly dissolves the drain cover and SCP-153 will position its own mouth in its place, which it then is able to camouflage as the missing drain cover almost perfectly.

Once SCP-153 has taken this position, it is virtually impossible to distinguish it from the original or discern that anything has changed.

SCP-153 will then lie in wait until it detects that someone has entered the shower or bathtub.

Once the unsuspecting person has begun to bathe, it will very quickly emerge from the drain, latching onto the victim's face, most likely in order to prevent them from calling for help.

It then begins to rapidly secrete more of the same acid that it used to dissolve the drain cover.

With how effectively it was able to dissolve metal, it's no surprise that SCP-153 is able to quickly produce the same effect on its victim.

Their skin, muscle, and bone will all be almost immediately liquefied, allowing SCP-153 to feed on the slurry.

And the Drain Worms feed extremely quickly as well.

After just several minutes, basically nothing will remain of the person who stepped into the shower, and 153 will retreat back into the drain, leaving no signs that it was ever there save for the missing drain cover.

The SCP Foundation became aware of this anomaly following multiple mysterious missing person cases that all had one key element in common, each was reported as having disappeared after entering a bathroom to either shower or take a bath.

The Foundation soon discovered that large populations of SCP-153 instances were living in the sewers beneath several major American cities, and immediately began enacting containment procedures.

The Foundation collected as many specimens as they could find and brought them to Bio-Research Area-12 where they keep them contained in 10 by 10 by 5 meter tanks that are kept partially filled with sewage and other organic material for them to feed on.

Of course it is of the utmost importance that these containers are never connected to any other plumbing systems, either internal or external.

With several specimens contained, the Foundation began researching the creatures in order to hopefully better understand them and how they were able to develop such complex hunting techniques.

Research was also approved to find out whether they could be used as a sort of waste disposal system in certain extreme circumstances, such as with SCP-2717, a mass of living animal tissue that has grown to line nearly 4 kilometers of sewer pipes beneath Amsterdam.

A small number of SCP-153 instances were approved for release into the wild in order to test whether they could stall the spread of 2717, however this experiment was halted following some disturbing new reports.

More missing person reports came to the Foundation's attention that bore the hallmarks of an SCP-153 attack, but these new reports were not limited to people who vanished after bathing.

It now appears that SCP-153 has further adapted, and has begun to emerge not just from showers and bathtub drains but now also from sinks, and yes, even toilets.

The Foundation is unaware of just how many instances of SCP-153 continue to exist in the wild, but there's no doubt that many continue to live and hunt undetected in sewers around the world.

This anomaly, which has been classified as Euclid, is taken very seriously by the Foundation, and any reports of people who go missing from bathrooms are immediately investigated for signs of SCP-153.

Field agents are to be equipped with infrared and ultraviolet sensors which can bypass SCP-153's camouflage, and if specimens are able to be captured alive, then they are to be brought to Area-12 for further research.

But don't bother worrying too much the next time you step into the tub.

If you've been targeted by SCP-153, there's not much you'll be able to do anyway, and your worries will soon be going down the drain, along with whatever remains of you.

20. SCP-015 PIPE NIGHTMARE

Three SCP Foundation agents stand before a large warehouse.

Their mission is simple.

Enter the building, find the observation unit that has gone missing inside, recover the data from it, and leave.

It should be easy.

But the rundown structure they're standing in front of is no ordinary building.

This… is SCP-015.

The leader of the group, a large, muscled man who goes by the codename of Agent Six, slides open a large door on the front of the warehouse, and immediately the whole group is struck by a sight that makes them reconsider just how easy this mission is going to be.

In front of them is not a wide-open warehouse floor but a cramped tunnel leading deeper into the building.

The group has a job to do though, and so the three head inside, Agent Two first, followed by Agent Lon, the data specialist, and finally Agent Six, the expedition leader in the rear.

As they enter the narrow hall of pipes, the light from their flashlights plays off the floor, walls, and ceiling.

Flashlights are one of the only items allowed in SCP-015, and they reveal what the researchers had told them in their briefing, that many of the pipes aren't made of standard materials, but instead are all sorts of strange substances like wood, glass, or even bone.

The odd series of pipes have formed a twisting tunnel leading deeper into the warehouse.

The group must be careful since the floor is uneven, with pipes occasionally sticking up out of the floor like tree roots, ready to trip the unobservant.

The three follow the corridors of pipes along the path that they each had to memorize.

As they come to branching paths, Agent Two speaks the series of turns they must take aloud.

Left.

Left.

Right.

Left.

Right.

Right again.

Straight.

Right.

And so on as they go deeper and deeper.

They'd have to follow the directions exactly if they hoped to reach the place where the Modular Robotic Vehicle should be.

Left.

Straight.

Straight again.

Right.

Just a couple more turns and they'd reach the point where the MRV had sent its last signal before going offline.

As they walk though, they find that some of the passageways are getting more difficult to pass.

The pipes have closed in at certain points, choking the already small tunnels down to mere crawlways.

At one particularly narrow point where the group must get down on their bellies and pull themselves along the ground.

After Lon and Two exit the tight passage, Agent Six suddenly calls out to the two agents ahead of him.

"What is it, what's wrong?"

Two asks.

"I'm stuck," comes from the response from Six.

Lon and Two grab Six's arms and begin pulling.

With a loud grunt from all of them, Six finally comes free.

His pant leg is shredded from the thorny wood that one of the pipes in the narrow tunnel is made from, but he's free and they can continue on.

Finally, after what seemed like an hour of walking, they finally find it.

The Modular Robotic Vehicle that had been sent in to investigate the current state of SCP-015.

There's something very strange about the robot's condition though.

It looks like it has been speared right through its primary observation unit.

A smooth black pipe that appeared to be made of dark fabric had pierced the vehicle right through its camera, but the lens didn't appear broken.

Instead, it looked as if the pipe had somehow connected with it, docking inside the lens housing as if the two parts were made for each other.

Other pipes had protruded from the floors and walls as well, snaking into open spots on the vehicle, and lifting it up a foot off the ground.

They looked over the robot which was held helpless in the air, its wheels slowly spinning as its internal battery ran down.

The agents walked around the MRV examining it, looking confused about the fate that had befallen it.

Six suddenly broke the silence.

"Well?

What are you waiting for?"

Lon wasn't sure what to do though.

As she got closer to the robot, she noticed that a foul-smelling substance was dripping from the pipe that had merged with the camera.

Her job was to remove the data from the MRV but they also had strict orders not to damage anything in SCP-015.

So what was she to do about the robot?

Wasn't it technically a part of SCP-015 now?

She was worried if she removed the data cards then SCP-015 might… well she didn't know exactly.

Six didn't buy it though.

The researchers may have told them that 015 "reacts" but he could see now that it's just a bunch of weird pipes.

Maybe it grows or moves a bit, but how would it even know they were there?

It hadn't shown any signs of sentience, let alone sapience.

He wasn't going to hang around in here any longer than he had too though, and if Lon wouldn't get on with it then he would.

Six moves to the MRV and flips open the data cover on its side.

More of the fetid liquid pours out but he ignores it.

Lon and Two both look at each other, did the other hear that too?

It sounded like steam venting from somewhere deep inside SCP-015.

Six doesn't seem to have heard it and begins to remove the thin data cards from the MRV.

With the data now recovered, he decides to see if could free the vehicle from the pipes.

It wasn't necessarily a mission objective, but why let good Foundation property go to waste when it's right here in front of them?

Six pulls first at the MRV, then the pipes that were running into it, but he can't

get it to move, it's completely stuck, seemingly fused to the pipes.

"Come on, we've got the data, let's get out of here," Two says.

But Six isn't done trying.

He sets his flashlight down and uses both hands, pushing against the wall of pipes with his foot to gain additional leverage, when suddenly there's a creaking sound.

"Ha!

I think got it - "

But Six was mistaken.

It wasn't the sound of the MRV coming free that he had heard, but the sound of the floor underneath him giving way.

Six falls into the floor up to his armpits and the other two agents rush to help him, but as they do they notice the glow and immediate burst of heat coming from the hole.

Thickly flowing molten glass begins to fill the hole and Agent Six cries for help as they desperately try to pull him free.

His cries turn into screams of desperation as they each grab an arm and after a struggle, finally manage to free him and drag him from the hole.

Six is no longer screaming as he is pulled free though, his eyes and mouth are locked wide in sheer panic.

Lon is now the one who starts to scream as she realizes that they have pulled only the top half of Agent Six from the hole the fiery pit.

The bottom half of his body is completely gone, burned away by the heat of the liquid glass.

There's no time to be shocked though, because pipes begin to hiss and ping all around them.

A wooden pipe above Two and Lon suddenly bursts, sending a cloud of dust flying into their faces.

It's powdered glass, and it starts to pour out of the broken pipe, covering what's left of Six completely.

Two spits out a thick stream of blood, his mouth shredded from the glass particles, as Lon desperately tries not to rub them deeper into the cuts in her eyes.

They both know they can't stay here though.

They have to run.

The pipes are deafening as they move as quickly as they can back the way they came.

It sounds like a train is barreling through the building.

They're surrounded by chaos.

Boiling chemicals pour out of one pipe.

Tiny slicing rose thorns spray out of another.

They come to a crawlway that's just a couple feet wide, but it's their only way forward and they have no choice but to enter.

Two dives in and starts crawling.

Lon is hesitant, but a blast of steam from a pipe near her head convinces her she has no choice and she follows after him.

Two wriggles through the narrow passage and is surrounded by more sounds of pipes creaking all around him.

Each one seems like it might burst and pour who knows what deadly substance onto him.

But he has to suppress his fear and keep moving forward.

Finally, he emerges into a wider hallway.

He turns and looks back at the hole.

Lon should have been right behind him, but there's no sign of her.

He sticks his head back in and calls for her.

There's no response but he can hear her still in there, somewhere in the dark, struggling.

He has to help her.

Two gets back into the passage and starts crawling.

She couldn't have been that far behind him.

Probably just around the next turn.

But as he crawls around the bend there's nothing there, just another wall of pipes.

The passage has been sealed up.

It's a dead end.

He presses his ear to the wall and can hear Lon screaming on the other side.

He hits his flashlight against the pipes in anger.

The pipe shakes for a moment then bursts, spraying out a black liquid that covers his hand.

It's some kind of corrosive acid and he screams as it burns through his gloves to the flesh beneath.

He quickly crawls backwards out of the narrow tunnel and emerges back out into the wider passage.

Two cradles his hand, trying not to look at the exposed bone.

"I'm sorry!" he cries as he runs through the tunnel of pipes towards what he hopes is the exit.

"I'll get help!

I'll come back, I swear!"

Lon can't hear his promises though.

She heard what she thought was a pipe burst followed by Two's cries, but she doesn't know now if he's dead or alive.

She decides she has no choice but to go back the way she came.

Maybe there's another way out, but after moving just a few inches her feet touch a solid wall.

She's trapped in a space no bigger than a coffin.

She feels around but there's nothing here in the dark, nothing at all, just smooth, fuzzy, warm pipes.

No wait, there is something, a gap in the ceiling.

But it's just the open end of another pipe, and now there's something dripping out of it.

Droplets of whatever the substance is land on her face, and then a full stream of liquid pours out onto her.

She coughs as it gets into her mouth but then realizes that it's sweet.

It's… honey.

At least it wasn't molten glass or deadly acid.

Maybe she could even survive for a time on the liquid, until another expedition team came to rescue her.

Her brief moment of hope is cut short when she realizes that the pipe isn't stopping, and that she's already lying in an inch-deep pool of honey.

Lon beats on the walls and ceiling as the honey continues to rise around her and screams for help.

She tries to plug the pipe with her fingers but it's no use, nothing can stop more and more of it from pouring out.

The honey continues to rise around her, and all she can do is scream and claw at the pipes that have created her tomb.

She presses her lips to the ceiling in an attempt to gain one last breath before the honey completely fills the space.

Her final choking gasps are sickly and sweet as the honey fills her lungs.

Agent Two keeps running through the tunnel of pipes.

His hand no longer hurts at least, either from the shock or from the fact that all the nerve endings had been burned away.

The horrible sounds coming from the pipes seemed to have stopped too.

Maybe he really would make it out of this alive.

Lon might have found another way out too.

There's no telling how many routes through this maze of pipes exist.

He would probably exit the building to find her outside waiting for him.

Poor Agent Six though.

He never had a chance after opening that cover on the MRV.

His thoughts are abruptly interrupted though when his foot catches on an unseen pipe and he falls forward onto the floor.

Or rather, he should have fallen on the floor.

Instead, a pit opens up in the ground leading to a steep, sloping floor of pipes.

He screams and tries to stop himself, but the slick liquid covering everything makes it impossible for him to slow his descent and he begins to slide down the pipes.

His dimming flashlight shows what seemed to be an endless tunnel of pipes stretching down into the dark.

The tube of pipes twisted this way and that, slamming him into the walls on either side, tumbling him head over feet.

And the descent never seemed to end.

He screamed until his voice went hoarse, then gave out entirely.

He didn't have any way to mark the passage of time other than when his flashlight finally started to flicker and then dim before finally dying.

He slid down the endless tunnel of pipes for what felt like days in the darkness, far deeper than they physically should have been able to go.

When the friction of the pipes began to tear his skin away, it was almost welcome.

At least there would finally be an end.

Following the loss of the SCP-015 recovery team, the data on the Modular Robotic Vehicle was deemed non-vital and no further expeditions were authorized in order to try and recover it.

SCP-015 is a mass of pipes, vents, boilers and other various plumbing apparatus that have completely filled an otherwise non-descript warehouse located in a major American city.

Any time the warehouse is not being directly observed, the pipes will begin to grow, filling nearly all of the available space in the building but also trying to connect to other nearby structures through the sewer and other subterranean infrastructure systems.

The current best estimate of Foundation researchers is that the building contains over 190 kilometers of pipes, which range from just 2.5 centimeters to over 1 meter in diameter.

While some of these pipes will look new, others have the appearance of being rusted or damaged, with many showing signs of leaking.

The pipes are made of a strange assortment of materials as well including bone, wood, steel, pressed ash, human flesh, glass, and granite.

Oddly, no pipes composed of lead, PVC plastic, copper, or any other material one would normally expect to be used for the production of pipes have been found.

But by far the strangest anomalous quality of SCP-015 is that it appears to react to aggressors.

Should the building detect that personnel inside of it are carrying tools, or if they make any attempt to either damage or repair any of its pipes, they will trigger an immediate reaction.

Pipes near the offending subject will often burst, spraying them with a variety of liquids that have included oil, mercury, rats, a species of insect not yet identified, ground glass, seawater, entrails, and molten iron.

More and more pipes will continue to burst around the subject until they either retreat from SCP-015 or are killed.

SCP-015 was discovered by the Foundation after reports that pipes emanating from a warehouse had mysteriously started to connect to multiple other nearby structures, with no obvious answer for how or why they had suddenly begun emerging from the structure.

The pipes were eventually able to be cut back and are now solely within the warehouse once again, but the human cost of containing SCP-015 has been high, and so far eleven SCP personnel have been killed in their interactions with the anomaly and an additional twenty are still missing.

All of the missing are presumed to also be dead, though there have been reports of banging and screaming coming from within the building that may indicate they are still alive in some form.

SCP-015 has been classified as Euclid, and because the building itself is impossible to move, it has been effectively contained on-site.

The Foundation maintains a gap of at least two meters around the warehouse, and no structures are allowed to be built that make contact with the building's outer walls.

Should any protrusions from SCP-015 be detected, the pipes are to be immediately capped and sealed.

Internal exploration of SCP-015 is permitted with approval from senior staff, but following numerous losses within the site, expedition teams must consist of three members all of whom are equipped with safety lines and GPS tracking.

The teams are not allowed to bring any hand or power tools with the building, nor are they to attempt any repairs or maintenance of any kind while inside.

There's no need to enforce these rules though, seeing as SCP-015 appears more than happy to terminate the offenders itself.

The SCP Foundation contains many anomalous locations though SCP-015 may just be one of the strangest.

But decide for yourself by comparing it to SCP-024, another abandoned building with secrets of its own to be found inside, and don't forget to subscribe and turn on notifications, so you don't miss a single anomaly, as we delve further and further into the SCP Foundation's classified archives.

21. THE DRINNER-SCP 4910

"Tell me if it starts to hurt," the dentist says before reaching into your mouth with a pair of orthodontic pliers and starting to pull your front teeth back into place.

Evidently, your screams aren't enough of an indication of the extreme pain you feel because he doesn't stop pulling.

After what feels like hours of excruciating oral surgery, you're finally standing outside the dentist's office texting with a friend.

"Come on, show me.

It can't be that bad," reads the message from your friend.

You're nervous to send her a picture though since you have a small crush on the girl and you don't want her to see you in this state.

But after she asks you again you decide to take a quick selfie and send it to her anyway.

You snap a photo of your mangled mouth and jaw.

The mess of wires had to be hastily applied to move your remaining crooked teeth back into place with globs of fast hardening epoxy and the result looks like a low-budget horror movie prosthetic.

You send the message and wait.

You watch the dots appear that indicate she's writing a response, then watch as they disappear without a reply.

You sadly slip the phone back into your pocket and begin walking away.

As you make your way home with your head hung in shame you keep your mouth shut tight.

You don't want any passersby to see what you've become.

You decide to detour through the park to avoid any people as much as possible and as you walk, you decide to stop at a picnic table next to a small pond.

You sit at the table and watch the ducks mill about in the water.

"They have it so lucky," you think.

"Ducks never have to worry about their teeth getting knocked out by a baseball and leaving them looking like a monster."

The ducks suddenly all start moving away from your side of the pond, eventually taking flight and leaving completely.

You get the sense that they're trying to get away from something and you turn around, but there's nothing behind you.

"Oh, it must be me," you think.

But then you get the sense that there is something behind you and turn again, still though, there's nothing.

It's just you, the picnic table, and the empty pond.

You turn back to watch the still water but you can't shake the feeling that there's someone behind you and turn again.

"Hello?

Is anyone there?" you ask but no one answers.

You turn back to the pond and - You scream in fright at the thing standing before you and fall back off of the picnic table.

You get up out of the dirt and you don't wait to stick around to see who or what this thing is.

You start to run as fast as you can but you immediately hear it chasing after you.

Instinctually you take out your phone and start trying to take pictures of whatever it is that's behind you.

You know no one will ever believe you and you want some evidence of this, this... thing.

You manage to snap off a couple of pictures but you can hear the creature gaining on you.

You scream as your mouth begins to ache.

Perhaps running this soon after your surgery is causing your damaged teeth to shift, and the pain is intense.

It starts to feel like your mouth is full of jagged rocks, but you can feel that it is your teeth pushing out and stabbing into your mouth.

You take one last picture before the creature leaps on you, sending you both to the ground and your phone tumbling into the dirt.

Early the next morning, a police perimeter has been set up in the park.

The detective arrives and walks past the traumatized looking jogger who must have been the one that discovered the grisly scene.

An officer guarding the site lifts up the police tape so the detective can enter the crime scene that surrounds a body lying under a white sheet.

The detective asks the officer if they've found anything yet and the office hands the detective a plastic bag containing a dirty cellphone.

The detective puts on a latex glove and removes the phone from the bag.

The screen is cracked but it still works.

There's numerous messages on the screen that look like they're from someone trying to apologize for not responding sooner, then asking where the phone's owner is and if they're mad at her.

The detective opens the phone's camera app and starts looking at the last photos that were taken.

It's a strange series of pictures.

They seem to all be selfies that a young man was taking as he ran through the park.

It almost appears as though there's a figure behind him but it's hard to tell.

There's a foggy white vignette on the pictures that gets worse the further he looks, slowly closing in until the last photo is nothing but a blurred milky white screen.

The detective flips the phone over and looks at the lens which he can see is completely covered in a hard white substance.

The detective places the phone back in the evidence bag and kneels down next to the body.

The police officer turns away, he's already seen the victim and doesn't need to again.

The detective pulls down the sheet to reveal a truly shocking sight.

The boy's mouth is a mess of teeth, far far too many teeth.

There are teeth growing out of every part of his gums at horrible angles, filling his mouth and jutting out at painfully odd angles.

Who could have done this?

What could have done this?

The local police department may not have had any idea what the state of this victim meant, but the SCP Foundation did, because they had seen the same occurrence dozens of times before.

In fact, they had seen it happen so many times that they had classified this anomalous entity as SCP-4910, but it had already earned a much ominous nickname within the Foundation.

It was known as...

The Grinner.

Very little is known about SCP-4910, and eyewitness accounts of the creature are all extremely brief, due to those who have interacted with it quickly succumbing to its effects.

What is known is that SCP-4910 is a quadruped, and appears to be made partially, or perhaps entirely, out of teeth.

Those who encounter SCP-4910 quickly experience its primary anomalous effect, which is that it causes the extremely rapid overproduction of teeth in its victims' mouths.

Existing teeth will quickly increase in size, protruding farther out of the gums than should be able, while new teeth will begin to sprout from any available space in the mouth including the roof of the mouth and underneath the tongue.

These new teeth will completely fill the mouth, which almost immediately inhibits their ability to speak or vocalize at all.

The creature will then use this opportunity to attack and incapacitate the victim, before starting to feed.

Further adding to the mystery of SCP-4910's appearance comes from the effect it has on any nearby recording equipment.

Cameras and other devices that come within SCP-4910's proximity will have their critical components compromised by a sudden appearance of a layer of dentin, which is the calcified material that partially makes up teeth.

Interestingly, SCP-4910 seems to possess some level of intelligence, as it appears able to differentiate between normal civilians, who it hunts for sustenance, and members of organizations that seek to hunt down and contain or harm it, which it uses for an even more nefarious purpose.

While the exact mechanics are still unclear, it seems as though SCP-4910 is able to "infect" certain anomalous organization members with its ability, causing them to act as a vector for the effect, who then spread it to even more victims.

This effect is, of course, of great concern to the Foundation, and containment protocols for infected victims have been hastily put into place.

Should a member of staff begin bearing a grin with too many teeth, or multiple tooth-filled smiles, they are to be immediately immobilized by any means necessary, though preferably with a firearm that allows one to keep an appropriate distance and hopefully prevent any further spread of the effect.

The infected individual is then to be doused in a hydrochloric chemical compound that will reduce the afflicted to a pulp-like substance.

Once this pulp is no longer animate, it can be transferred to the closest incineration site for disposal.

Should a member of personnel have an interaction with SCP-4910 and feel that they were exposed to its anomalous effects, they may be saved by taking immediate medical action.

Oral surgery to remove the additional teeth has been found to be effective when the procedure is undergone in the first one to two hours following exposure, though the victim will suffer lifelong permanent physical issues from the procedure.

Once three hours have passed, the effect will have spread to the rest of the body, with teeth appearing virtually anywhere.

Unfortunately for the victim, should the infection reach this point, pain management has been shown to be ineffective, and there is nothing that can be done to alleviate their suffering save for termination.

SCP-4910 remains at large and has been given the Keter classification.

Mobile Task Force Epsilon, codenamed "Tyrfing Black" is the only MTF authorized to respond to sightings and they have been given permission to engage the creature and utilize lethal force if necessary due to the danger this anomaly presents specifically to the SCP Foundation.

22.SCP-3899 -THE NIGHT HAULER

You're on your way home from work after having just finished working a double shift.

It's late and the interstate is completely abandoned, no cars visible either in front or behind you.

It's only about a twenty minute drive but you know you're going to struggle to stay awake, even in this old beater that shakes and rattles as it travels down the long, straight road.

The rattling causes a piece of tape to fall off of the gauge cluster, revealing a lit "check engine" light beneath.

You grab the tape and put it back over the light, covering it once again.

There, good as new.

You turn on the radio and it comes to life for just a moment before dying.

You slap the radio and it blinks to life for just a second before dying again.

You're about to slap it again when you notice lights in your rearview mirror.

And more than just a pair of headlights, it's a whole wall of lights.

They're getting closer and quickly too.

Before you know it, they look like they're barreling down on you.

But then, they suddenly go black, blinking out of existence.

"Did that trucker just turn off his lights?" you think but you have no time to dwell on the thought because the sound of an explosion suddenly causes you to scream in fright.

It sounds like lightning has struck just inches from your car.

The inside of your car suddenly lights up with fire and smoke.

Has your engine exploded?

What's going on?

No, it's not coming from you, it's coming from… next to you.

You don't know where it appeared from, but next to your car is now a massive semi.

At least you think it was a semi.

The smoke is so thick it makes you cough and you quickly can't see.

You lose control of the car and slam on the brakes, but you can feel yourself going off the road.

As the smoke finally clears up inside of your car you can see… the moon.

It's at this moment that you realize you're no longer right side up as the car flips and tumbles through the air.

You open your eyes to find that you're still buckled into your seat.

You release the seat belt and drop to the roof of the car.

You crawl out to find that your car slid to a stop, upside down, several meters from the road.

You look around, and far off in the distance you can see it, the semi that ran you off the road, driving at an almost impossible rate of speed off into the night.

You look back at your car, which is completely totaled, and wonder what you're going to do now.

It's late the next morning when you finally get back home.

The police did not seem to believe your story about the magically appearing semi-truck causing your single car accident, but they did at least give you a ride back home after administering a sobriety test.

You enter your small studio apartment and look around at the sparsely decorated room, wondering how you're going to pay rent next month if you can't get to your job.

You go to the fridge and open the door, but there's nothing inside except for a carton of milk that's well past its expiration date.

You open it and take a whiff but this is too far gone even for your state of desperation.

You close the fridge and lean on the door, trying to figure out what you're going to do.

You're so deep in thought that you barely notice the mail being pushed through the slot in your door.

You decide to go pick it up, even though you know it will only be bad news.

And you were right, bills, bills, and more bills.

First, second, and final notices.

You wonder if you've ever had a piece of good news show up through that slot in your door.

What's this though?

The last piece of mail is a battered and folded envelope that looks like it's been used and repurposed many times.

It feels thick and heavy, but there's no information on it at all, it's completely blank.

You open the envelope and your eyes light up.

Inside... is money.

It's a stack of crinkled, old bills, different denominations all in a random order, but there's a lot of them.

There must be over a thousand dollars here!

And there's something else too.

A note.

You unfold the creased and dirty piece of paper to see a simple message that looks like it was hastily written in black crayon.

All the note says is "SORRY BOUT LAST NIGHT!!
HOPE THIS HELPS COMPADRE."

You flip the note over and look in the envelope again but there's nothing else other than the wad of cash.

The apology note may have been unsigned, but you weren't the first to receive something like it, and you would be far from the last.

The SCP Foundation, though, knows exactly who sent it.

This was a message from SCP-3899, also known as...

The Night Hauler.

SCP-3899 is a black, Peterbilt 379 semi-trailer truck with an attached trailer.

But as you no doubt have determined, this is no ordinary truck.

SCP-3899 has the anomalous effect of appearing seemingly at random, upon stretches of highway within the continental United States and usually at a considerable distance away from any other motorists.

The truck will manifest already in motion, traveling within roughly three kilometers per hour of the posted speed limit, but it will not stay at this speed.

Once SCP-3899 has appeared, it will almost immediately begin accelerating, and the speeds it can reach are truly staggering.

Despite appearing to be a normal truck, SCP-3899 is able to reach impossibly fast speeds, and it's been observed traveling at over 420 kilometers per hour, or 267 miles per hour.

As SCP-3899 flies down the road, it will attempt to avoid other vehicles and roadside objects, and has even shown the ability to displace itself across short distances, which it seems to mostly do in order to avoid collisions with vehicles.

SCP-3899 will disappear and then immediately appear somewhere else, though always within 300 meters of its last location.

This reappearance will be accompanied by a thick cloud of dense, black smoke that lab tests have revealed to consist of a mixture of diesel fuel combustion byproducts, volcanic ash, and trace amounts of unidentified human blood.

The anomalous truck will only appear at night, and will demanifest completely once it encounters direct sunlight… or if it causes an automotive accident, which it has done plenty of times.

In one particular incident, undercover SCP Foundation agents working within the Virginia State Department of Transportation became aware of reports of a large black truck appearing on a particular stretch of interstate that had caused multiple accidents.

They were able to track down and locate one of the victims of these incidents, a woman named Martha Lewis, who they soon brought in for questioning under the guise of it being a police investigation.

The agents questioned Martha on her experience, and she explained her own interaction with the black, semi.

She said:

"It's all still clear in my head.

I'm driving down I-64 on my way home and the sun had just gone down.

There's no other cars and I'm about to take my exit, when out of nowhere this huge truck just… appears, right next to me.

There was a bunch of smoke, like it was on fire or something, and the sound was like a bolt of lightning had just struck right next to me.

It all happened so fast.

All the smoke clouded my windshield and before I could really process what was happening, I was plowing right through a concrete divider and into some trees.

I think I passed out.

When I came to, there were paramedics and cops.

They took me to the hospital."

The agents asked if anything happened after that and she said there was one other odd thing.

When she left the hospital and went home there was a letter waiting for her, but it didn't have a return address.

Inside was a large amount of US currency in a random assortment of denominations, with many of the bills appearing wrinkled and worn.

There was a note in the envelope too which read:

IM SORRY.

DIDNT MEAN NO HARM.

FOR THE DAMAGES.

GET Y'ALL A NEW RIG AND DRIVE ON!!!

Later Foundation analysis of the document revealed that the note was written with a piece of charcoal on non-anomalous notebook paper.

Now you're probably asking yourself the same question that SCP researchers had.

Just who is the driver of SCP-3899 that apparently wrote this odd note and also paid for the damages they caused.

The operator of the truck, which has been designated as SCP-3899-1, is a very mysterious figure.

Observers who have been able to get a brief glimpse inside of the truck as it moves past them at a rapid speed have described the driver as looking only like a silhouette of a slightly overweight male wearing the type of headwear that is typically referred to as a "trucker hat."

Some reports have also alluded to the presence of what appears to be smoky, tentacle-like appendages within the cab, though all further efforts to determine the exact physical characteristics of 3899-1 have failed, as the truck has proved resistant to any kind of outside scanning equipment.

Most of what is known about the driver has come in the form of direct communication, though not in the form of interviews or any other sort of face to face interaction.

No, while SCP-3899-1 has never been willing to stop and have a discussion with Foundation agents, it does seem more than willing to speak with anyone and everyone in its immediate vicinity over Citizens band, or CB radio, which is a type of shortwave person to person communication system that is popular with many long haul truckers.

In one particular instance, an SCP Foundation helicopter happened to be traveling above a stretch of road where SCP-3899 appeared.

An agent within the helicopter began communicating with the anomalous trucker, first asking for their callsign, to which SCP-3899-1 replied:

I'M THE NIGHT HAULER AND I'M COMIN' IN HOT!

I KNOW Y'ALL CAN FEEL THIS SPEED!

After adjusting their volume to compensate for 3899-1's loud response, the agent asked if the entity could explain where they came from.

3899-1 answered with:

I ROLL WITH THE WIND!

MY WHEELS SING SWEET LOVE TO THE BLACKTOP!

I'M FILLIN' Y'ALL'S VEINS WITH ROAD SALT AND EXHAUST AND THE SMELL-A BURNIN' RUBBER!

AIN'T NO BOTHER WHERE I'M FROM, WE ALL GOTTA LIVE FOR THE RIDE AND DIE FOR NOTHIN'!

"I see," the agent responded, before asking "Are you 'hauling' anything in particular?"

SCP-3899-1 came back with:

Ain't you listenin', girl?

Are you seein' this?

What I got is pure rattlin' salvation, eighteen wheels at a time!

When y'all's roads is choked, when the ways is blocked and y'all's speed is all dead and gone, I'm droppin' this load and we'll all be drinkin' gas and breathin' smoke!

The agent didn't understand though, and asked again who they were and what they wanted.

3899-1 replied:

THIS IS FOR THE SOULS OF THE ROAD!

FOR THE LONG NIGHTS AND DEAD ENGINES AND EVERYONE TRY'NA PUT THAT HORIZON UNDER THEIR WHEELS!

I AM THE ROAR OF HOT IRON!

I AM SCREAMING FREEDOM!

I AM THE DEATH OF ALL BARRIERS!

THIS RIG AIN'T GOT NO QUIT, HONEY!

I DO NOT STOP!

CAN YOU FEEL THE RUMBLE?

CAN YOU SEE THE FIRE AND SMELL THE BURN?

I KNOW YOU CAN, I CAN TASTE YOUR HEART AND I KNOW YOU WANT TO FLY APART WITH ME!

When the agent began to answer in the affirmative that they could indeed "feel the rumble," seemingly caught up in the excitement of SCP-3899-1's proclamation, the investigation was quickly halted and the helicopter broke off from its pursuit.

Following this incident, the potential memetic influence of communicating with 3899-1 is under investigation.

SCP-3899, being currently uncontainable by any conventional means, has been classified as keter.

Upon reports of it manifesting, all CB radio transmissions emanating from the truck are monitored by nearby Foundation listening posts for attempted contact by SCP-3899 to civilian recipients.

Any individuals who were contacted are to be administered Class B amnestics, as are any eyewitnesses of the truck itself.

All information about SCP-3899 is to be suppressed, and a disinformation campaign is active to make all reports of a mysterious truck that can appear out of nowhere and move at impossible speeds seem like nothing more than an urban legend.

Just what is SCP-3899?

Is the driver some sort of anomalous ghost?

Or perhaps an old, eldritch god, a manifestation of freedom and perpetual motion given physical form as a diesel powered behemoth on the highway.

Perhaps the answer to that question... is up to you.

23. SCP-4595 WITCH

All he could see were glimpses, flashes of movement, but he could clearly makeout that there was a girl.

He could see the man walk up behind her and slip a bag over her head.

There was a struggle.

A body being dragged through the dark, and then the sound of a shovel scraping against the hard dirt.

The body is thrown into the shallow hole, and as the dirt begins to rain down on her face, her eye opens up.

The boy's eyes open too and he sits up with a panicked jolt.

Shaky and covered in sweat, he looks around his dark room and realizes that it was only a dream.

The entire morning as the boy gets ready, rides the bus, and sits through school, all he can think about is the dream… and the girl.

A group of teenage girls are out for a ride in one of their father's sports car convertible.

They're having too much fun, and driving much too fast down the dark country roads.

It doesn't take much, it never does, just the shadow of an animal bolting across the road but it's enough to make the driver jerk the wheel, causing the car to lose control.

All of the girls scream, but none more than the one who is tossed from the sliding, spinning car.

The girls stand around their dead friend and make a solemn pact, no one will ever know that she was with them.

But what will they do with her?

One of them points towards the woods and everyone turns to look at the dilapidated shed.

As the girls, now dirty from their long night of digging and then filling a hole, emerge from the shed into the dim morning light, none of them are aware that beneath the dirt, the girl is still breathing.

The boy gasps for air and struggles in the dark.

He throws the blankets off of him before realizing that he is safe in his own bed.

Another breakfast, another ride to school, another day of classes where the boy can think of nothing but the girl from his dreams.

Who is she?

He's never seen her in his life, he's sure of it.

But then why does she keep appearing in his dreams?

The boy is snapped out of his deep train of thought by the teacher slapping his desk and he apologizes before focusing on his studies once again.

The look on the woman's face is a mix of sadness… and annoyance.

She doesn't know how much longer she can go on like this.

It never stops, how can someone cough so much?

The woman sits in her chair and tries to push away the same thought that comes to her over and over… that it would be better for both of them if it would just end.

The girl coughs loudly in her bed.

The disease has ravaged her lungs and it takes all of her willpower not to scratch at the burning, itching sores on her face and chest.

She looks towards the door with dazed eyes and sees her mother enter the room.

She's carrying a tray with soup just like she always does at this time, even though she has no appetite at all.

As her mother gets closer she can see that the tray is empty… and it isn't a tray in her hands, it's a pillow.

The girl can barely muster a scream as the woman places the pillow over her daughter's face.

As the mother walks out of the old shed in the backyard and towards the house she stops for a moment.

Can she hear the sound of coughing coming from the shed?

That morning at breakfast, the boy's father tells him in no uncertain terms that he doesn't want to hear any more about the girl.

It's just a dream, and he needs to put it out of his mind.

What he needs to be focusing on is school.

The note from his teacher said that he isn't paying attention in class and if that keeps up he's going to have much bigger problems.

The boy promises, no more about the girl.

As the boy stares out the bus window, it isn't his fault that thoughts about his dream rush into his head.

Because as the bus drives along the country roads he catches a glimpse of something down a long, tree covered driveway - it's the house from his dream.

The shed door opens with a creak, allowing a sliver of light from the full moon to fall inside.

The boy enters the shed as quietly as he can and goes inside.

He soon emerges with his bike, and a shovel strapped to his back before riding away from his own backyard into the night.

The boy stops his bike at the bottom of the driveway leading up to the old, abandoned house.

He rides up the drive and doesn't even consider stopping at the house, his destination is somewhere else.

The boy lets his bike fall to the ground in the backyard and stares at it... it's the shed he's seen so many times before despite never seeing it in person.

It's dark and quiet, the shed silhouetted against the large, bright moon.

He approaches the only door on the small shed and reaches for the handle.

It opens with a loud, rusty squeak.

The boy takes out a flashlight and turns it on, illuminating the shed's interior.

Inside is nothing except for a wooden bench sitting on the dirt floor.

But wait, there is something else.

A spot on the ground appears different, blackened, almost as if it were burned.

This is the spot though.

This is the place the boy keeps seeing in his dreams.

He knows she's down there.

She needs his help.

The boy thrusts his shovel down into the dirt but it doesn't even scratch the surface.

The ground is cold and hard.

He strikes down again and the shovel pierces into the dirt.

The shovel suddenly falls to the ground though as the boy begins to cough.

He drops to his knees as the coughing becomes a fit.

He can't stop and now he can't breathe.

It feels like his throat is filling with... something.

He falls to the ground, still coughing as he feels whatever is filling his throat and lungs moving and vibrating.

With a final, great hacking cough he unleashes a swarm of creatures from his mouth.

He lies in the dirt, struggling but unable to get any air, as the buzz of thousands of locusts drowns out his final noises.

It's no surprise that what this young man ran into wasn't a dream at all, but an interaction with an anomaly that has since been classified as SCP-4595, but also has the quite simple and appropriate name of... Witch.

SCP-4595 is the designation given to a small room located inside of a woodshed, that is itself found behind a home near the town of Jasper, Indiana.

The house appears to have been abandoned for some time, and there are no reliable records of who the home's most recent or original owners were.

The only item inside the woodshed is a simple, rough hewn, wooden bench, though at the time of the anomaly's discovery, two other objects were found as well.

The first was a small shovel, the type that might be used for gardening.

The shovel appears to be ordinary in every way, except for the very tip which has what looks to be a bloodstain on it, though tests have been able to retrieve any genetic material from the discoloration.

The second object was a small human skeleton.

The body of the deceased person was removed from the woodshed, and an autopsy revealed that it had belonged to an adolescent male, roughly 11 to 13 years old.

While the exact cause of death was unable to be determined, it is extremely likely that it was due to the anomalous effects that SCP-4595 produces, but more on those in a moment.

Further examination of the woodshed reveals that the word "WITCH" has been scrawled on the door with charcoal, though it is unknown who wrote the message and whether it is meant to serve as a warning or has some other purpose.

It is highly likely though, that the word is referring to the final element of SCP-4595, the body that is buried beneath the woodshed's dirt floor.

Ground penetrating imaging tools were brought in to investigate the shed, and researchers discovered that underneath one portion of the floor that appears to have been scorched at some point, a body is buried roughly one meter beneath the surface, which has since been designated as SCP-4595-A. Scans have revealed the body to be a humanoid figure,

vaguely feminine in appearance.

It's limbs are twisted in a painful, and unnatural manner, and there are several large wounds present on its face, chest, and neck.

But perhaps strangest of all is that despite evidence at the site pointing to the location not having been disturbed for many years, the corpse buried beneath does not seem to show any signs at all of decomposition, still appearing as it most likely did at the time it was interred in the ground.

You are most likely asking yourself why the SCP Foundation has relied solely on subterranean imaging in order to assess the state of SCP-4595-A, and why they don't simply dig up the anomalous corpse.

The reason why they haven't is due to the anomalous effects present at the site.

Testing on SCP-4595 has concluded that anyone who enters the shed and remains there for any substantial amount of time will begin to experience a number of effects.

First, they will start to feel paranoid, getting the impression that someone is watching them.

This purely mental effect is quickly followed by a physical one, where the individual's skin will start to itch.

Those who linger in SCP-4595 long enough will eventually begin to violently scratch at themselves in an attempt to relieve the itchiness.

These effects, while very uncomfortable, will eventually subside if they leave the location, and it is very likely that they are meant to serve as a warning of what will happen if one partakes in the most dangerous aspect of SCP-4595, which is disturbing the body buried beneath it.

Anyone who attempts to impact SCP-4595-A by attempting to dig it up or otherwise remove it from the location, will quickly experience a horrendous anomalous effect.

The individual will soon find that they are experiencing a shortness of breath, and soon will begin coughing and choking, and be unable to breathe at all.

This is due to a phenomenon in which any empty space in their chest cavity, lungs, airways, stomach and intestines, will completely fill with Schistocerca gregaria, better known as the desert locust.

The insects will continue to appear within the individual's body until they expire, a process that typically takes mere minutes.

Any locusts that manage to escape the individual's body, most often through the mouth and nose will disappear into a vapor that quickly dissipates the moment they cross the threshold of the woodshed's doorway.

So far, no method has been determined that can prevent any of SCP-4595's effects, and for the time being, no personnel are allowed to enter the anomalous shed except for testing purposes, but even in those cases the disturbance of SCP-4595-A is not allowed.

Due to the relative ease with which the Foundation can secure the site and is able to prevent anyone from entering, it has been classified as Safe, with the additional disruption class of Dark and the risk class of Warning.

Just what is SCP-4595?

Is the SCP-4595-A body a victim?

Doomed to an eternity beneath this ramshackle shed?

Or is it a monster?

Sealed away for some unknown purpose, the only warning for us to stay away being a single word on the door?

Maybe one day, we'll finally know the answer to why SCP-4595 is only known as the Witch.

24. GODZILLA SCP? SCP -2954 LOOPING KAIJU KILLING

A gigantic monster stomps across the land, with nothing able to stop its rampage except for - "Come and eat!" cries out a voice and the monster suddenly stops and falls to the side.

The child picks up his toy and runs back to where his mother and father have spread out a picnic lunch.

As they eat, the boy asks his father about the nearby buildings, a series of six identical structures, each of which is a small, rectangular building with a satellite dish on top of it.

The weathered buildings look like they have been out here for some time, and the father tells the boy that he isn't sure exactly what they are or what their purpose is, but that they were probably built during the war.

"What war?" the young boy asks.

"The Pacific war," his father answers.

"What was that?"

"It was a war fought by many countries of the world."

"Why did they fight?" the boy asks.

"Well, there were a lot of reasons."

"What were some of the reasons?"

The father has played this game many times before and he knows if he doesn't end this line of questioning now, that he'll never be able to eat his lunch.

The mother, sensing the same, tells the boy that if he wants to he can go and play with his toy some more.

The boy doesn't need to be given the option again, He quickly gets up and grabs his toy monster before running off to play.

"Don't go too far!" his mother calls out as she watches her son head in the direction of one of the buildings.

The boy stops in the shadow of one of the large satellite dishes and sits down in the grass to resume his monster's path of destruction across the countryside.

As the monster moves through the tall grass though, the shadow he is sitting in suddenly starts to shift.

The boy looks up to see that the satellite dish on top of the building is moving.

With a groan, it begins to turn and change its angle.

And it isn't just the one on the building closest to him that's moving, he can see that each of six satellite dishes are doing the same thing.

They're all turning to point towards the same spot on the horizon.

The boy squints in the sunlight and sees what they're all now directed towards.

Off far in the distance… is a real monster.

It's a massive looking creature, a huge, half fish, half lizard covered in scales and spiky fins.

It must be at least 50 meters tall or more, and it's coming straight towards him.

The boy can already hear the sounds of its giant webbed feet stomping and shaking the ground, and as it gets closer its high pitched shrieks and cries become audible too.

Adding to the cacophony, an air raid siren begins to wail, followed by the sounds of gunfire, the marching of hundreds of boots, and the roar of engines.

The boy looks around but he doesn't see any of it.

It's just him, the buildings, and the monster.

The boy can't run though, he's frozen in fear.

All he can do is watch as it swipes at trees and power lines, knocking them down with ease, all while getting closer and closer.

The satellite dishes finally finish their slow alignment and there's a loud humming noise, followed by a loud, cracking sound as each one emits a bright beam of electricity at the monster.

The creature stops its assault and howls in pain as the six satellites focus their beams on it.

The beams disappear and the monster appears stunned, but then it looks up and continues to come forward, this time even faster than before.

The monster is only hundreds of feet away now and the boy doesn't know what to do, he's too scared to even scream for help.

He closes his eyes and starts to cry when he's abruptly lifted into the air.

The boy opens his eyes to see that…

It's his father!

He picks up the boy and starts to run as fast as he can.

The boy can see over his father's shoulder that the monster has not changed its course to follow them, it seems to still be focused on the building he was playing next to.

The monster finally reaches the building and begins swiping at it, tearing it apart as the other satellites slowly realign, all pointing at the creature once again.

The sound of the invisible army increases and the monster reels as if it is struck by unseen weapons.

It suddenly rears back in pain as an artillery shell appears just feet away from it before exploding in the creature's face, but nothing seems able to deter it and it keeps clawing at the building with the satellite dish.

The father finally reaches the mother who grabs the boy and embraces him tightly.

There is a loud noise and the family turns to watch as the monster finishes destroying the building and turns its attention to one of the others.

But then the dishes unleash another blast of electricity at it with a thunderous crack.

The creature howls in pain as it stumbles and falls to its knees.

It is struggling to get back up when yet another blast hits it and it falls to the ground.

It breathes a couple of final, labored breaths before it closes its eyes, its enormous tongue lolling out of its mouth.

The creature is finally dead.

A loud, celebratory cheer goes up in the empty field from what sounds like hundreds of people as the creature begins to slowly fade from view before eventually disappearing completely.

Meanwhile, all the family can do is stare in amazement at the bizarre scene they have just witnessed.

The extremely strange events that just befell this average family may sound like the plot of a movie, and in some ways, it was, because this is SCP-2954, also known as…Looping Kaiju Killing.

SCP-2954 is an anomaly that consists of several distinct components.

The first, SCP-2954-1A, are the six large structures that resemble buildings with satellite dishes which are located near a now deserted rural town in Japan.

The word "resemble" is very important, because these are not actual satellite dishes, but instead appear to be nothing more than facsimiles of real ones.

The interior of the SCP-2954-1A buildings lack all of the mechanical components one would expect to find inside, and instead contain only a crude rope and pulley system, which control the satellite dishes on the building's roof.

Despite their lack of internal machinery, the satellite dishes are nonetheless somehow capable of discharging powerful electric arcs of energy, which they only do when confronted by an SCP-2954-2 instance.

SCP-2954-2 refers to creatures which have a mix of reptilian, amphibious, and fish-like traits.

They are always fifty to sixty meters in height, and most of their body is smooth and blue-gray in color, except for their scaled underbellies, which are red.

Both their back and forearms have large spiny fins and SCP-2954-2 instances walk upright on two legs, though they are always hunchbacked.

Their mouths are also always agape, and are capable of spitting a highly corrosive liquid.

These creatures appear during a period of time that have been designated as Tsuburaya Events.

These events, which start every seven days, consist of a single instance of SCP-2954-2 manifesting near the SCP-2954-1A buildings before it begins destroying its surroundings.

The buildings will then activate, turning their attention on the creature and firing their electric arcs at it in an attempt to stop its rampage.

This will cause SCP-2954-2 to focus its attention on one of the buildings, which it will then try to destroy.

As it does so, the sounds of weapons being fired, vehicles moving, and orders being shouted in Japanese can be heard.

This phantom army, which has been designated as SCP-2954-1B, is only heard not seen, and there are never any physical signs of their fight, save for the creature's own reactions to the weapons, and the occasional artillery shell that will materialize in midair before striking it.

During these Tsuburaya Events, the SCP-2954-2 instance will always destroy at least one of the satellite dish buildings, and various other explosions roughly equivalent to what would be expected from small vehicles being destroyed will also be seen as it fights back against the 2954-1B army.

Eventually, the combined assault of the 1A and 1B forces will be enough to overwhelm the creature, and it will collapse, grow transparent, and eventually disappear completely.

A disembodied cheer will be heard, presumably from the 1B army, and any damage to the environment including the 1A buildings will be reversed.

But what is the cause of this endless cycle of destruction and restoration?

Where do the creatures come from and what do they want?

And who is the invisible army that always stands ready to fight back against the rampaging monsters?

The answers to those questions may have been discovered while exploring the area where the Tsuburaya Events take place.

There, in another small abandoned building, SCP Foundation agents discovered a trove of objects that may shed some light on just what these creatures are.

The objects located included various movie posters, film reels, and documents that appear to be related to the production and distribution of motion pictures.

The posters seem to depict creatures quite similar to the SCP-2954-2 instances, and the title of the poster when translated from Japanese reads: Fukaeru's Assault!

When agents viewed the footage on the film reels, they found that it depicted a scenario quite similar to the Tsuburaya Events.

Also of interest are a series of notes found within a filing cabinet inside of the building, with several being of particular note.

The first, when translated from Japanese, reads:

Our sponsor gave twenty monsters to shoot.

We'll pick the best footage.

The second which is dated to 1974 says:

Filming completed.

Don't forget: call our sponsor to say further shipments are unneeded.

The third and fourth are both addressed to what may be the film's producers, and they read:

Do you need more Fukaeru?

We can resupply until you're satisfied!

And:

You have not replied for a while!

Regardless, we will send another shipment.

Happy filming!

But perhaps strangest of all, is that there are multiple similar versions of the last note, and while the oldest is dated to 1972, additional instances continue to appear to this day, with new letters sporadically manifesting inside of the filing cabinet.

The obvious danger that is caused by a rampaging, 50 meter tall monster is clear, and this anomaly has been classified Euclid as a result.

Though since the creature is inevitably always killed by the SCP-2954-1 forces, containment is instead focused on keeping the public away from the area.

Guards have been stationed around the area to prevent civilians from entering during Tsuburaya Events, and any members of the public who do manage to witness an event are to be administered Class A amnestics.

What is the origin of these Looping Kaiju?

Did someone attempt to harness an anomalous source in order to produce special effects for their film?

If so, were they killed by their own creation before being able to turn it off?

Leading to a never ending cycle of attacks?

While we may never know the answer for sure, at least the result is entertaining, provided you keep your distance that is.

25. SCP-056 A BEAUTIFUL PERSON

The gleaming steel scissors glide effortlessly through the sheet of red material, slicing through as if nothing was there.
The blood red fabric parts to either side.
A pair of hands pick up one of the pieces and hold it up into the air.
The man admires his handiwork before draping the cloth on a dress form and pinning it in place.
Although there are many tables in the large room with sewing machines and mannequins next to them, they're all empty.
The man works all alone in the big room.
And it is impossible to notice that he's an incredibly handsome man too.
So good looking that no matter your preferences, you can't help but stop and take notice of his perfect facial features, his slim, fit physique, his lithe, dextrous hands.
He brushes a strand of dirty blonde hair away from his vibrant blue eyes and takes a pin out of his mouth before adjusting the fabric just a millimeter more before sticking it in place.
The man steps away from the dress form and admires his work.
There, absolutely perfect.
There's no doubt that this will be the closing look of the upcoming fashion show.
Another masterpiece.
Just like him.
But that doesn't mean that he's finished.

There's still much to be done and he goes back to work at his table, sewing bits of fabric together to create embellishments for the opulent, couture gown.

He's so focused on his new design that he doesn't notice the fashion house's operating manager in the hall outside of the workroom.

The manager points through the glass window in the door and tells the two police officers with him that this is the man they are looking for.

There's been a number of tragic and mysterious crimes involving people connected to this fashion company, and the police have finally closed in on a suspect.

Well not the police exactly, but two SCP Foundation agents posing as police officers.

The Foundation became suspicious after learning that there had been several missing persons, murders, and mental breakdowns, all of which involved people connected to this one company.

And even more specifically, they were all connected to one man.

There was plenty of evidence that something more than just regular criminal activity was happening here.

Something strange was happening, something anomalous.

One of the police officers nods at his partner before gesturing for the manager to leave. It's always better not to have civilians present during a containment.

The incredibly handsome man still hasn't noticed his guests in the hall, remaining completely absorbed in his work, and he doesn't even look up when the two agents burst into the room, both with guns drawn, not taking any chances.

"Freeze!

Drop your weapon!" one of the agents shouts, but the beautiful man doesn't respond, and just continues snipping away at fabric with his scissors.

"I said freeze!" he commands again, and this time, the handsome man at least appears to have heard them, finally stopping his work.

He slowly looks up with his piercing eyes to gaze at the men who have intruded into his creative workspace.

"Drop your weapon, now."

the agent tells him.

The man looks over at his hand which still holds the large pair of scissors and smiles.

He gently places the scissors down on the table, careful not to let them touch the expensive cloth that is rolled out before him.

"Now put your hands up!"

This time there's no response and the man grips the edge of the table, smiling, and stares into the eyes of the agents, first one, then the other.

"Hands up or we'll be forced to shoot!"

The smile slowly leaves the handsome man's face.

"Will you excuse me for one moment," he says, though with no hint in his voice that

it's actually a request.

The agents seem unsure of what to do, both of them appear taken aback and confused by his nonchalant attitude.

The handsome man turns away from the agents and quickly steps behind a dressing screen that's been setup near his work table.

As he walks behind it, he doesn't break his stride at all, he simply passes behind the screen for mere seconds, and steps out on the other side.

Only once he steps out, it isn't him anymore.

The man that emerges from behind the screen is a completely different person.

Where once he was slim, graceful, clean shaven, and dressed in a fine suit, now he is heavy and muscled, like a professional football player, with a thick beard, and dressed as if he's a member of a SWAT team.

Before the agents can even react to the bizarre metamorphosis, the large man charges them and begins attacking.

He snaps the neck of one and plunges the scissors he snatched off the table into the other's neck.

More SCP containment specialists, these ones dressed in tactical gear with no attempt made to disguise themselves as everyday police, flood into the room and open fire, but the man who looks like a Navy SEAL picks up the fallen agent's guns and begins firing both at the same time.

He outguns and outmaneuvers the agents, effortlessly rolling behind cover while constantly firing, taking out agent after agent.

Screams fill the air, both from the dying SCP agents as well as the civilians who are struck through the walls by the onslaught, including the manager who had snuck back to the door window to watch what he thought would be the snobby, handsome man being taken into custody.

The window behind the special ops soldier explodes and two SCP agents rapel through, catching him by surprise and knocking him to the ground.

It takes even more agents rushing in to hold the man down as he struggles and screams like a wild animal, breaking one of their jaws for good measure before they're finally able to subdue him and confine him with heavy duty straps.

When all is said and done, seventeen agents and ten civilians have lost their lives, but the anomaly has finally been contained.

Once it is taken to a secured location it is given a new designation, SCP-056, but the site staff soon give it a new nickname, calling it simply… A Beautiful Person.

SCP-056 is one of the most deceptive, and one of the most dangerous anomalies known to the SCP Foundation.

It is a being whose size, gender, and appearance can all vary in an instant, and which will change in response to its environment.

The form it has most commonly taken while in contrainment resembles a man who appears to be in his mid twenties.

His exact looks will vary slightly but he will always be what could be described as incredibly handsome, at least by traditional societal standards.

His clothes will change as well to be a style similar to those of other people around him, though they will always be of a higher quality and more aesthetically pleasing than anyone nearby is wearing.

While that appears to be SCP-056's preferred form, it's far from its only one.

In addition to the young man, it has also been observed taking on several others including a woman with a striking resemblance to Hollywood actress Scarlett Johansson, a form it took when walking past a group of a younger female staff; a male bodybuilder who could bench press over 250 kilograms, which was 30 kilograms more than the strongest security guard stationed at the Foundation site; it took the form of a female doctor who was measured as having an IQ score 30 points higher than any on site researchers; as well as non human forms like a large, well groomed labrador retriever when it was exposed to another researcher's dog, and an extremely aesthetically pleasing couch when left alone in its own containment chamber.

These changes from one form to the other occur whenever people lose focus on the subject, something that seems to happen when new people are exposed to SCP-056.

And once they lose focus, it's able to change in appearance virtually instantaneously.

Attempts to film the transformation have resulted in the recording equipment exhibiting the same effect, seemingly "losing focus" and being unable to see exactly what happens when SCP-056 changes from one form to another.

It's clothing will change along with its bodily form, though so far it hasn't been observed manifesting weapons or other tools.

Great efforts have been made to determine SCP-056's "original" form, though so far these have all been met with failure.

When placed within an empty concrete cell and placed under constant video surveillance, the cameras experienced the same loss of focus that others did, and then were met with a rather surprising figure left in the room.

SCP-056 had taken the form of a video camera, similar to the one being used to record it though a slightly more advanced and expensive model.

Additional attempts were made to discover its true form, this time without direct observation equipment, with researchers instead making use of passive scans that could detect changes to lifeforms.

When they left SCP-056 alone and monitored it using these tools, what they found was… nothing.

There was no detectable body temperature, heartbeat, or even weight.

It appeared that when not observed, SCP-056 simply ceased to be.

Those who have personal contact with SCP-056 often report that the anomalous entity makes them feel substandard, or jealous, as if they can't measure up to it, yet at the same time will seem to seek its approval.

This extends to SCP security staff, who will express a desire to follow its commands, while researchers will try to argue with it, something that usually results in them leaving its containment cell feeling as though they were outwitted by its itelligence.

And SCP-056's expert communication abilities seem not to be limited by complex subjects or language barriers.

Research has shown it to be fluent in at least 200 different dialects, and it has exhibited an expert level of knowledge in such varied topics as fashion, automobiles, theoretical science, sports, and a multitude of others, all of which it will usually show a greater knowledge of than the person it is conversing with.

And despite leaving the conversations feeling dejected about their own abilities, those who talk to it will almost always express a desire to speak with SCP-056 again, as if they can't resist being made to feel inadequate by it.

A number of tests were then performed to discover just what form SCP-056 would take when presented with various situations, and the results were rather interesting.

In the first, a male Class D personnel was given a knife and told to try and attack SCP-056.

056 quickly took the form of a young, fit man who was able to effortlessly disarm the attacking D Class and killed him with the knife instead.

In another test, a female D Class entered its cell not with a weapon, but with a bottle of expensive wine.

They were met with SCP-056 in the form of a young, beautiful woman, who accepted the wine but upon trying it, spit it out in the D Class's face and sent them away.

Next, researchers sent two D Classes in at the same time, one male and one female, with no specific orders at all.

SCP-056 appeared as a beautiful woman in a well tailored business suit who proceeded to examine both the D Classes, pointing out their each and every physical flaw before sending them too on their way.

Researchers then tried sending ten Class D personnel into the cell, all of whom were male and who had expressed a romantic preference for females.

SCP-056 appeared as an especially beautiful female in a low cut red dress.

056 didn't interact with the group in any way, but after ten minutes the D Classes began to look uncomfortable.

Soon an all out brawl broke out between the D Classes as they violently assaulted each other, apparently for SCP-056's approval.

056 seemed to watch the melee with pleasure for several minutes before calling an end to it and sending them all out.

A member of staff then volunteered to be tested with SCP-056, a level 4 personnel who was regarded as being especially beautiful herself.

She entered SCP-056's cell, where the anomaly took the form of a similarly beautiful, professional looking woman, and the two proceeded to have a conversation, discussing various advanced personnel management techniques.

Their discussion seemed amiable, but after ninety minutes, the staff member appeared to become infuriated with SCP-056 and quickly left the room.

While no crosstests with other SCPs have yet to be performed, when asked about other anomalies, SCP-056 shows a rare instance of vulnerability, expressing hatred towards them and even occasionally... fear.

SCP-056 has been relatively benign in its time in SCP containment, seemingly content to spend its time around Foundation staff.

It's been allowed to have a cell of its own choosing, as well as pick its own furnishings, which have tended towards expensive and fashionable decor.

Security staff assigned to guard it are equipped with high powered tranquilizers and any staff that exhibit mental irregularities after extended exposure to SCP-056 must undergo immediate psychological examination.

It has frequently asked for access to the internet, and when asked why it desires that, SCP-056 responded that the Foundation was "unable to provide it with enough sycophants", and that it "wanted the whole world to know its face."

Needless to say, its request for internet access was denied, and the anomaly which has been classified as Euclid, continues to be securely cut off from the general public and remains in Foundation containment.

26. SCP-2640 GHOST LIGHTS

"Just a little further" your friend says. They're leading your group, and as you all emerge from the woods your flashlight illuminates a tall, chain link fence with barbed wire strung across the top.

"How are we supposed to get over that?" another of your friends asks, and the group's leader has just the answer. They point their flashlight several yards down where you see a large pine tree that has fallen over onto the fence, creating a bridge that you should be able to shimmy along to get over the barrier.

You and your group of friends take turns climbing over the toppled tree before dropping down on the other side of the tall fence.

After dusting yourselves off, your group walks further into the clearing until you come to an old set of railroad tracks that are rusty and look like they haven't been used in some time.

"Well?" one of your more incredulous friends asks, "what's supposed to happen?"

The group's leader explains that "if we're lucky, we'll see it."

"See what?"

"The ghost light."

They go on to explain that on certain nights, a mysterious light will appear in this very clearing, wandering the area around the railroad tracks.

"What is it?" you ask.

Your friend tells you that many years ago, maybe a hundred or more, this was once a bustling and busy stretch of railroad. One night, a Union Pacific worker came out to check a portion of the tracks that were supposedly damaged. The worker went out into the night with his

dim lanter, and he walked along the tracks until he stopped in this very clearing.

He spotted what looked to be damage to one of the rails and bent down to examine it. No one knows why he didn't hear the train barreling towards him, or hear its whistle cry out in the night, but the man would never hear anything again, as BAM! The train took his head clean off!

Now, with only his lantern to guide him in the night, the headless railway worker wanders this clearing, still searching for his missing head.

"That's a stupid story," one of your friends says. "How could someone not notice an entire train?"

"I don't know, but it's true."

"No it isn't."

As the two go back and forth, you suddenly notice something in the distance. "Um, hey, look over there."

Everyone follows the direction you're pointing and sees it. A dim ball of light hanging in the air.

"See," your friend says, "I told you it was true."

He steps towards the ball of light and as he does it actually moves, drifting back at the same rate he comes forward, as if to maintain the exact same distance. When your friend takes a step back, the light moves just the same.

"Look, over there!" you say, "another one!"

What's going on? Were these the ghosts of multiple headless rail workers? All searching for their missing craniums? This light is brighter than the other though, and rather than maintaining a set distance from your group, it's slowly moving towards you.

"What do we do?" one asks.

"I don't know!" the leader says, "I've never dealt with a ghost before!"

The light continues to move towards your group and no one knows what to do. Frozen in fear, you watch as the light passes straight through you, and your friends start to scream as it is absorbed into your chest. Their cries become muffled though, sounding to you as if they're underwater. And your hearing isn't the only thing that feels that way. Your whole body suddenly feels as though you're submerged in liquid. You can't breathe and you thrash at the air, trying to swim but nothing is there. You scream and choke, then fall to the ground as the ball of light passes through you like you weren't even there, leaving you in the dirt gasping for breath.

Your friends rush over to help you up, asking what happened, but there's no time to explain because two even bigger, brighter lights have appeared. You're terrified of what they might do to you but before you can even think about running a voice calls out from the darkness.

"Stop right there!"

The two big balls of light are headlights attached to the front of a black SUV, and a pair of angry looking armed guards have just gotten out of it.

The last thing you hear is one of the men say "I can't believe we have to deal with this," before you feel the sting of a dart hitting your thigh and your vision goes black.

You open your eyes to find that you're sitting in your own car with your group of friends.

They too appear to have been asleep and are just waking. You're parked on the side of the road next to a thick forest of pine trees and the sun is just starting to rise.

"What were we supposed to do again?" one of your friends asks from the backseat.

"I don't remember," you say, "but the sun is coming up. Let's get out of here."

And you drive your group of friends back home with no memory of the previous night's events.

This group of teens were quite lucky. What they thought was little more than an urban legend known as the The Gurdon Lights, was actually a mysterious and dangerous anomaly which the SCP Foundation knows much better as SCP-2640.

SCP-2640 is a temporal anomaly that is found within a 5000 square meter area near the town of Gurdon, Arkansas. The area is densely covered with pine trees, with the only man made object found within it being a set of railroad tracks that bisect the area.

Of most interest within SCP-2640 though, are the strange entities that manifest inside. Designated as SCP-2640-1, these entities are floating orbs of light that are capable of appearing alone, or in groups, though no more than twelve at once have ever been observed manifesting at the same time.

Their light will vary in intensity, from 75 to 450 lux, which is roughly equivalent to the range of light produced by standard light bulbs, and the color is always a bluish white.

The lights will normally be seen to travel slowly within SCP-2640, though they have been observed moving quite quickly on occasion, with the quickest ones having been measured traveling at speeds of up to 60 kilometers per hour.

There is also a connection between the luminosity of the entities and their behavior. Those measured at less than 150 lux will not interact with humans, instead maintaining a distance of at least 20 meters from the nearest observer at all times.

Attempts to move closer will lead to the entity moving away at the same rate, ensuring that it maintains the same 20 meters of distance at all times. On the opposite end of the scale, those that are closer to 450 lux are very active, and will approach and even interact with humans.

In some instances, the brighter SCP-2640-1 entities will actually pass through solid objects, including people, which leads to a very strange sensation for the person involved.

When this has occurred, the subject has described a sensation of "being suspended in liquid" or "floating in a swimming pool" despite there being no outward physical changes to them.

This feeling of being in water will start the moment a 2640-1 entity makes contact with their body and will cease once it is no longer touching them.

The SCP-2640-1 entities appear bound to the SCP-2640 area, and any that approach the boundaries will slowly dim until they disappear completely.

In order to better understand the nature of SCP-2640, and specifically the 2640-1 entities found within, an expedition into the area using D Class personnel was authorized.

The three Class Ds were equipped with special equipment capable of measuring the relative reality distortion in a given area, and told to follow along the railroad tracks that run within SCP-2640, with orders to report anything they experienced that was out of the ordinary.

As they progressed deeper into SCP-2640, their equipment detected significant reality distorting effects, and just as they did, the SCP-2640-1 entities began appearing. Despite being quite scared of what they perceived as "ghosts" the Class D personnel were under strict orders not to run. A 2640-1 that was on the brighter end of the scale approached one of the D Classes and passed through his body, leading him to experiencing the sensation of being underwater and, since he was unable to swim, made him believe that he might drown. The entity passed harmlessly through him and he was left with no lasting injuries, at least not any physical ones.

After this test and given the extremely high reality distorting effects that were detected in the area, it was theorized by researcher Dr. Connors that SCP-2640 might be one of the strongest temporal anomalies on the planet. His report goes on to hypothesize that SCP-2640-1 are actually lifeforms from another time period that we can see visually, due to this anomaly, yet cannot interact with lest we cause irreparable damage to the time/space continuum.

Dr. Connors also noted that the area of SCP-2640 appeared to be slowly growing, and in order to prevent further spread the installation of several Xyank/Anastasakos Constant Temporal Sinks or XACTS was authorized.

And it was a good thing that the XACTS were installed, because there was soon an incident that would prove how necessary they are.

In a debriefing after said event with Tony Hargrove, a Level 03 Tech Support Staff, the SCP Foundation learned a horrifying reality about the true nature of SCP-2640.

Mr. Hargrove explained that he was sent into SCP-2640 in order to assess the damage to Foundation assets after a major tornado had passed through the area. He explained that while power was still running to the site, one of the XACTS had been damaged and needed to be replaced, so a maintenance team was sent to install a spare that was kept on site.

As the maintenance team approached the area where the XACTS was no longer functioning, they reported that there were numerous 2640-1 instances out, more than they had ever seen before, and a higher concentration of the brighter instances than usual.

Soon after they reported this, Hargrove lost contact with the maintenance team and decided to go investigate himself. As he entered the SCP-2640 area, he saw something that he had never seen before. There weren't just a few more instances of 2640-1s than normal, but hundreds, maybe even thousands, floating all around him.

There were so many that they lit up the sky to the point where he didn't even need a flashlight.

Hargrove followed the same railroad tracks that the maintenance team had, and after walking several hundred meters he spotted something in the mud next to the tracks. It was the replacement Temporal Sink that they were supposed to be installing. And there was blood on it.

He realized that there wasn't just blood on the machine, but it was everywhere, covering the ground all around him.

Then he saw something else. An SCP-2640-1 instance near him, but different somehow.

"I can't remember how I first saw it," he said, "right behind the orbs, there was this spot where the rain just... wasn't. Like it was bending around some invisible mass, some great thing behind each orb. And once I saw it, I couldn't unsee it." Hargrove tried to step back away from the creature and fell into a ditch next to the tracks, clutching the XACTS in his arms as the creature seemed to swim towards him. As he lay still as he could in the ditch, he got the sense that this 2640-1 instance wasn't just randomly moving towards him, it was looking for him. As the void where the rain ceased to be swam over him through the air, he attempted to lie as still as he could, still holding tightly to the XACTS. The SCP-2640-1 instance turned and circled over him, like a shark searching for its prey in a cloud of blood, before gliding away into the trees.

At that moment, Hargrove knew that the SCP-2640-1 entities weren't what the Foundation thought they were. These weren't just beautiful balls of light that danced and played in the darkness. They were something else, something horrible, something dangerous. He also knew that his maintenance team would never be found, and that the ditch he was lying in that was slowly filling with rainwater was mixed with their blood. The SCP-2640-1s were hunting them, and they never had any idea.

Hargrove knew what he had to do. He crawled through the ditch, stopping any time a 2640-1 got near to him, holding his breath until long after it passed. It took hours of inching along on his belly in the water and mud until he finally reached the point where the damaged

XACTS was located. He managed to get the new temporal sink online and as it powered on, he watched as the 2640-1 lights around him slowly started to fade and then disappear once again.

The deaths of the four Foundation personnel who were on the maintenance team, as well as six other civilians who were killed, were attributed to the tornado, and Mr. Hargrove requested that he be administered Class B amnestics reassignment to a new location, both of which are pending approval.

The rail line that runs into SCP-2640 has been decommissioned, and a 3 meter tall electrified fence has been erected around the entirety of the area in order to prevent civilians from approaching.

No fewer that 8 Xyank Anastasakos Constant Temporal Sinks are placed in the surrounding area in order to prevent the further spread of SCP-2640, and a subterranean miniaturized pressurized water reactor has been installed on site in order to provide constant, uninterrupted power. The Disinformation Bureau has an ongoing dissemination campaign to further the notion that the SCP-2640-1 lights are nothing more than an urban legend, and should any civilians manage to witness them, they are administered Class B amnestics in order to keep this Euclid class anomaly a secret.

Just what is the true nature of SCP-2640, and perhaps more importantly, SCP-2640-1?

Is the breach of our reality a look into the past, when this area was covered by an ancient ocean?

Or a glimpse into the future? When the seas have swallowed it once again.

No matter which is the answer, the reality is that there is something there now, something that has managed to pierce the veil of time and make us its prey.

27. SCP-4419 THE BUTCHER'S CHARIOT

"Watch this!" the teenage boy says before jumping his skateboard up onto the stair railing.

His friends watch in amazement as he deftly guides his board down the long rail.

They hoot and holler in support until suddenly, the boy seems to lose his balance.

He falls from the rail and tumbles down the stairs of the large parking garage where they had been practicing their skateboarding tricks.

The boy hits the ground hard at the end of the stairs and all of his friends go quiet.

The boy is stunned but eventually he opens his eyes and stands up, but none of his friends can do anything except stare.

"Oh no oh no oh no" the boy says as he looks down at his arm, which is now bent at a ninety degree angle in a spot where no joint should exist.

The children watching all begin to scream, and one, unsure of what else to do, turns and runs.

"What do I do?

What do I do?"

the boy with the broken arm says to no one and everyone.

Luckily, one of the group quickly collects herself and steps forward to take control of the situation.

"Come on," she says, "we're getting you to the hospital."

The girl puts her arm around him on his non-damaged side and helps him to the street, where they have a stroke of good luck.

Parked just a block away, is an ambulance.

"Hey!" the girl cries out, waving towards the ambulance.

The paramedics inside must have seen her because the ambulance's lights immediately come on and it drives the short distance to them.

The ambulance stops and two paramedics quickly exit the vehicle.

The paramedics don't even need to ask what happened, they can obviously see from the unnatural angle of the boy's arm that he needs immediate medical attention, and they quickly place him into the back of the ambulance.

The girl begins to pull herself into the back as well, but is quite forcefully shoved back into the street.

"Patients only," is the sole response from the paramedic who pushed her before he slams the door shut.

The girl gets a brief look at her friend's frightened face through the back window as the ambulance speeds away.

Several days later, the children are sitting outside of the same parking structure, but none of them are in any mood to skate, all they can think about is their missing friend.

Neither the boy's parents, nor the police, have any idea what happened to him or where he went.

There's no records at any of the local hospitals of him ever being brought there, nor does there seem to be any evidence of this particular ambulance having existed at all.

No one even seems to believe the children that he got into an ambulance, the whole story just seems too far-fetched and outlandish.

But the children know what they saw.

As they discuss the events for the hundredth or perhaps thousandth time, one of the smallest of the group suddenly stands up and points.

"There it is!"

The rest of the group looks in the direction he's motioning and sees the same thing, it's the ambulance.

None of them know what to do as the vehicle flies past them, this time with no lights on, and comes to a stop a block away from where they first spotted it.

They watch as the two paramedics exit the vehicle and go around to the back.

It's hard to see from this distance, but it looks as though they took something out of the rear of the ambulance, something that requires both of them to lift, before dropping it on the sidewalk behind some trash cans.

The children watch as the paramedics get back into the ambulance and drive away, disappearing just as quickly as they appeared.

After a moment of shock, they all in unison begin running to the place where the ambulance stopped.

They come to a skidding halt just in front of the trash cans.

None of them can do anything except stare until they all break out into screams, one of the children turning and immediately running away.

And they have good reason to scream, because in front of them, is their friend.

His arm is no longer broken, appearing to have been somehow repaired in just a matter of days, but it is also no longer attached to his shoulder.

The boy opens his eyes as his friends scream and looks down to see that his arms and legs have been reattached at a new angle, jutting out from his back, leaving him standing on all fours, his face staring up at the sky like some kind of twisted animal.

What happened to this young man was tragic, but he wasn't the first victim of this strange malicious anomaly, and unfortunately, neither would he be the last.

Because this was SCP-4419… also known as…

The Butcher's Chariot.

SCP-4419 appears to be a seemingly normal vehicle, which resembles a standard ambulance, though the exact make and model varies between manifestations.

This anomalous ambulance will appear spontaneously in locations where a medical emergency of some kind is about to take place.

Just how SCP-4419 is able to predict where and when these events will take place is unknown, nor is it understood how it always takes the form of an ambulance that resembles one appropriate to the local area.

Once the medical event has occurred, whether that be a minor injury like a sprain or something more serious gunshot wound, SCP-4419 will quickly approach the injured individual.

Two individuals which have a humanoid appearance and are dressed in paramedic uniforms that are, just like the ambulance, always appropriate to the location, will exit the ambulance.

They will then secure the victim, using a stretcher if need be, and place them in the back of the ambulance.

While the individuals who emerge from SCP-4419 will, for the most part, act as though they are normal medical professionals, they will strongly resist any attempt to either impede them in their quest to secure the injured person, as well as prevent anyone else except for their target from getting into the back of the SCP-4419 ambulance, up to and including the use of extreme physical force.

As soon as the the paramedic appearing individuals have managed to secure the victim in the back of the ambulance, it will then quickly leave the area at a high rate of speed, and research has shown that as soon as it is out of observation, SCP-4419 will demanifest, along with whoever is inside.

But this isn't the end of what this anomaly has in store for its victim.

Between two and seven days later, the SCP-4419 ambulance will suddenly reappear at the same area where it picked up its victim.

The same individuals will exit the ambulance, and leave the victim somewhere nearby before getting back in the vehicle and leaving the scene once again.

The victim who is left behind, will always have suffered what can only be described as invasive bodily modifications.

Their injuries are so extreme that in most cases they should have resulted in the death of the victim, and yet they will always somehow still be alive.

While the exact form of modification will vary from victim to victim, there does appear to be some correlation between the original medical emergency and the resulting procedure, and the SCP Foundation has documented a number of encounters with SCP-4419 stretching all the way back to the early 1980s.

Some notable examples include one from 1983 in which a pedestrian who was crossing the street was struck by an automobile, resulting in them breaking their leg.

SCP-4419 was on site and quickly helped the man into the back of the ambulance.

06:39

When he was returned several days later, all of his limbs had been reattached in such a way that they were protruding from the front of his torso.

In another which occurred in 1994, a man suffered a broken jaw in a fight outside of a bar.

To no surprise, SCP-4419 was on hand and took the man away for treatment.

When he was next seen, his jaw had been permanently forced open, and a glass window had been installed in the back of his throat, which permitted direct viewing of his heart, which had also been moved to the back of the throat.

Unfortunately there was no way to reverse this procedure, and the man had to be euthanized.

In 2003, a husband and wife were in a car accident where they each sustained multiple broken bones.

When SCP-4419 dropped them back off, the two had been fused together at the back, and any bones that were broken in the crash had been removed completely.

When an elderly gentleman had a heart attack in 2006, he was picked up by SCP-4419 and returned with eleven new, non functioning hearts grafted inside of his body.

Attempts were made to remove these additional hearts through surgery, but unfortunately the man did not survive the procedure.

In 2008, a structure fire resulted in nineteen people suffering extreme burns.

Seven more injuries came when a crowd attempted to stop the SCP-4419 paramedics from placing all of the victims in the back of the ambulance, but they were unsuccessful in preventing them from leaving the scene with them.

When the group of victims was finally returned, it was as a single organism, a large solitary mass which twitches and shivers when physical contact is applied.

No method for euthanizing this organism has been able to be found, and currently they are stored inside of a tank at Site-31.

In perhaps the strangest sighting of SCP-4419, a US private was wounded while on patrol in Afghanistan and a military medical evacuation vehicle arrived to evacuate him.

Suspicious about the vehicle's sudden appearance and the forceful conduct of the medical staff, the private's fellow soldiers ended up opening fire on the vehicle.

They reported seeing a viscous black fluid leaking from the vehicle's surface, but they were unable to stop it from taking the injured private.

In a deviation from its normal behavior, the victim was not returned to the same place, and instead, appeared in the barracks the next day.

The victim had been broken down into a thin paste and was spread across the walls.

Agents were dispatched to secure what was left of the man, and they reported finding a still intact eyeball that dilated when they approached.

The collected viscera has been labeled as "remains" and placed in storage, but it is currently unknown whether or not the victim has truly expired.

Due to the danger SCP-4419 presents to anyone who suffers an injury, as well as its ability to appear virtually anywhere on the planet, it has been classified as Keter.

Containment efforts at this point are largely focused on maintaining information control and post-manifestation cleanup, as opposed to any attempts at physical confinement.

Anyone who witnesses an SCP-4419 manifestation is to be administered amnestics, and victims are to be treated in order to restore them to their original physical state as much as possible or euthanized when no viable medical treatments are available, with a cover story constructed in order to explain their death.

SCP-4419 is one of the most cruel and sadistic anomalies in the SCP Foundation's database, ranking right up there with the SCP-106 the Old Man.

Hopefully one day we will find a means to contain this brutal so-called medical vehicle, but until then, be careful if you suffer an injury and an ambulance is suddenly on hand,

you might come back changed in ways you never thought possible.

28. SCP-2678 A CITY ALL OF BLOOD

The single piercing, high pitched note echoes through the cathedral.
It hangs in the air as the boy sustains it for far longer than his small lungs should be capable of.

The boy is the star of the choir and is well known throughout his city and even beyond, and people come from far and wide for the chance to hear his perfect soprano voice.

But on this night, there are only a few people scattered amongst the many rows of pews to listen to the choir as it practices.

And for good reason, while the boy's lauded voice is as sweet and powerful sounding as ever, the choir itself is at its lowest point in recent memory.

This nadir has occurred because many of the other boys who used to sing in the choir…have vanished.

The choir finishes its song, that's all for tonight, and the boy's begin to put on their coats and gather their things from underneath their chairs.

The boy with the perfect voice feels something on his shoulder and spins around with a fright to see that it is just the hand of the priest who is also the conductor of the choir.

The priest is an old man with a deeply wrinkled yet kind face, and he reminds the boy that he is to head straight home.

The boy promises the priest that he will go directly to his house and the priest reassuringly pats the boy on the shoulder before walking away to give the same advice to each of the other boys.

The boy steps out into the dark cold night as the heavy cathedral doors shut behind him.

It's softly raining and he pulls his coat shut to try and keep out the damp and cold.

As the boy begins to walk he takes note of the closed newsstand across the street.

The day's papers are still hanging outside and tell of yet another boy who has gone missing, this one from the next town over.

There are still no leads in the cases and parents have been growing angry with the police over the lack of any progress.

As the boy walks down the darkened street he fails to notice the shadowy figure that has stepped out of a dark alley near the cathedral.

But soon he hears the sound of feet on the wet sidewalk behind him. He glances over his shoulder and sees that the figure is walking the same direction as him.

The boy looks back straight ahead, not wanting to draw any more attention to himself and tries to increase his pace.

As the boy walks, his well trained ears quickly detect that whoever is walking behind him has sped up as well.

The boy doesn't run but he feels a surge of real fear begin to rise inside of him.

The boy picks up his pace even more and again hears the person behind him increase theirs.

The boy is walking so fast now that if he went any faster he'd have to break into a run.

His house isn't far though.

He turns a corner and can see it, a quaint little home with warm light pouring out through the windows.

He knows that inside his mother will be standing in the kitchen cooking dinner.

He knows that inside is protection from the night and shadows.

The boy looks behind him and sees the figure round the same corner.

The boy can't wait any longer and he starts to run.

And he sees over his shoulder that the figure has begun to run as well.

The boy is sprinting as fast as he can, his feet kicking up water from the sidewalk.

He can hear the figure getting closer and closer to him, their long legs outpacing his own with ease.

He's so close to his house though.

He's so close to being dry, and warm, and safe.

He slides to a stop on the damp stones in front of the door and reaches out for the handle.

Inside the warm little house the woman cooking dinner is startled by the sound of the door suddenly bursting open.

She turns to see an empty doorway.

She steps out into the street but it too is empty, nothing present but the sound of the wind.

And the almost imperceptible sound of a single note being sung... a beautiful, high pitched note.

What happened to the boy who was once the shining star of the cathedral's choir?

And what of the other missing boys?

Where did they all go?

Perhaps, they went to SCP-2678, a mysterious spatial anomaly that is also known as… A City All of Blood.

SCP-2678 is an extradimensional space that so far is known to be accessible through exactly one entrance - a door in the basement of the Siena Cathedral in Siena, Italy.

Strangely, the extradimensional location behind the door is only able to be entered by individuals who hold what could be termed, traditionally Catholic beliefs.

Perhaps even stranger though, is that when it was first discovered, the door to the space was barred and a metal placard had been placed next to it that read "SCP Foundation Department of Abnormalities".

This might not sound especially odd, but it came as quite a surprise to the agents investigating it as there is no record of there ever having existed a Department of Abnormalities within the SCP Foundation.

Other than SCP-3790 of course, which is another padlocked room bearing a similar sign, but that file has been locked by the O5 Council and we will have to save our exploration of that for another time.

Back to SCP-2678.

Individuals who have Catholic beliefs that enter the SCP-2678 space find that they emerge into a small, tent-like structure that appears to be a sort of forward operating base that has been built around the freestanding doorway.

The outpost is abandoned but there still remains a number of strange objects including a biomedical laboratory-grade refrigerator containing numerous samples of blood and bone, various types of audio recorders ranging from old wax strip models to magnetic tape machines, and a computer terminal which when activated requests Foundation credentials.

However all attempts to access this computer have been met with failure, as it has rejected all attempts for reasons of "insufficient clearance."

Also found inside the outpost was the score for a previously unknown choral prelude titled "Sul Golgota" which when translated from Italian means "On Golgotha" with Golgotha being the name of the hill that Jesus Christ was crucified on according to the bible.

The last object found in the tent was a skeleton, though several bones were missing including the hipbone and both forearms.

Further examination of the skeleton revealed it to have belonged to a young male, though the exact cause of death was unable to be determined, nor was it clear whether the bones had been removed before or after the young man expired.

Upon exiting the outpost, visitors to SCP-2678 will find that they are on the outskirts of a gigantic city that is floating in the middle of a red-orange void.

The city is truly massive, having been measured at being over 300 square kilometers in size, and consisting entirely of cathedrals, palaces and churches all of which are in the Italian Gothic style of architecture.

A never-ending rain of a red liquid that was found to be human blood falls on the city at all times and has stained the buildings a deep red color, and while they appear at first glance to be made of marble, analysis has found that all the buildings are actually constructed of human bone, specifically bones belonging to human males aged seven to twelve.

Later tests of the material found within the forward outpost's biomedical refrigerator revealed the stored blood and bones to be samples taken from throughout the city.

No life has ever been observed within SCP-2678, though visitors have reported hearing a high pitched, discordant melody that seems to come from somewhere deep within the maze of structures.

All attempts to record the sound have failed, as all audio equipment malfunctions when within the space, and playback of recordings results in them having only picked up the sound of the blood rain falling at a very high volume.

This explains the various types of audio equipment found in the forward outpost which were likely used in unsuccessful attempts to record the music.

Attempts to trace the source of the melody through the labyrinth-like city will inevitably lead to the same building, which is an exact replica of the same Siena Cathedral that the entrance to SCP-2678 is located in, though it too is made of bone that has been stained red from the falling blood.

And while the outside of the cathedral perfectly matches its real world counterpart, the inside is a different story.

Inside the cathedral, one will find only a single, large pipe organ.

The pipe organ has had its longest pipes, the ones that produce the lowest notes, cut in half and the corresponding pedalboards torn out. Pressing a key on the organ will produce a note that mimics an adolescent male's voice, and each key has its own unique voice.

Just like with a normal pipe organ, a note can be sustained for as long as the key is pressed down, though after a time the voice emanating from the organ will seem to take on a panicked tone.

Attempts to determine just how the organ produces the notes have been met with failure, as the organ does not have a windbox, bellows, or blower of any kind which would normally move air through the pipes.

The organ has another effect within SCP-2678 besides just producing sounds though, as whenever a note is played, the rain falling outside will transform into regular water.

No matter how long the note is held and the now regular clear rain falls though, the buildings will never be washed and always continue to be stained red.

Tests were performed on the organ in order to determine just how long it could sustain a single note, and the C7 key was pressed for over 20 minutes, during which time the voice continued to sing out, becoming more and more stressed and panicked sounding as time went on.

Finally, at the 23 minute, the key itself splintered into pieces, permanently removing the ability to produce that note.

The splintered remains of the key were also observed to bleed for several days following this test.

Expeditions sent into SCP-2678 have resulted in agents appearing to undergo a number of behavioral changes that, at present, are hypothesized to come as a result of hearing the organ music within.

The psychological changes have included an increased appreciation for choir music, an ever stronger belief in structured religion, more trust in authority figures, less trust in those coming from a lower social or economic status, and a reluctance to report crimes committed by fellow members of the SCP Foundation.

These changes appear to be permanent as well, as there has been no evidence of them fading with time.

Unfortunately, little to no progress has been made in understanding the mysterious and unnerving space, nor what the presence of a Department of Abnormalities forward operating base inside could mean, and so for the time being, all further explorations within have been canceled.

The doorway in the basement of the Siena Cathedral has once again been barred with the entrance hidden behind a bookshelf, and the ease with which the extradimensional location can be contained by the Foundation has resulted in it being given the Safe classification.

What do you think SCP-2678 actually is?

Who built the strange city of blood and bone?

If it was built by a person at all.

29. SCP-181 LUCKY

"Twenty-three… bust" the dealer says before scooping up the cards from in front of the man who appears to be growing increasingly angry as his stack of chips increasingly dwindles in size.

Making matters worse for the man, are the cheers of excitement coming from the nearby craps table, where it seems all of the luck that he has lost has somehow been transported.

As the blackjack dealer once again reveals an ace and a king, another burst of noise comes from the craps game. "Seven again" the croupier cries before placing a huge stack of chips in front of the young man playing craps who seemingly can't lose.

The young man on the hot streak collects his winnings and walks happily through the crowded casino floor right past the fuming man at the blackjack table. The young man cashes in his chips and counts the large stack of hundred dollar bills given to him before tipping one to the woman working inside the cage. And this night is far from a rarity for this young man.

For his entire life, it's been as if he couldn't lose. He's not strong, fast, or especially smart, but he's always managed to excel thanks to his one incredible gift - his never ending good luck.

The young man soon recognized his ability to consistently beat games of chance and went to the one place in the world best suited for his skills - Las Vegas. And Vegas has been very, very good to him. He lives in an expensive hotel room right on the strip, drives fancy cars, and treats himself nightly to lavish dinners and shows. It's all possible because no matter what the game is, it's as if he can never lose.

The young man is in the middle of another hot streak, or rather, continuing his never-ending hot streak, this time at the roulette table. "How does he keep doing it?" someone in the crowd asks as the man hits another number straight up, paying out thirty-seven to one on his bet.

The crowd cheers and slaps the man on his back as a crowd has formed who are following along with his every bet, piggybacking on his luck as much as they can. The man is just about to place another large bet when he's suddenly interrupted by a strong hand gripping his upper arm. The young man turns to find a large, toothy grin staring back at him. The smiling man continues to hold onto the young man's arm as he explains how impressed the casino is with his skill. He must be the luckiest man they've ever had the pleasure to have visited their casino, and the fact that he's been able to sustain that same run of luck night after night has been truly awe inspiring.

The young man thanks him for his kind words and tries to turn back to the table but finds that the man won't let go of his arm, gripping it even tighter now than before.

"We've been so impressed, in fact" the man tells him, "that the owners of his casino have requested the chance to meet with you."

The young man looks down at the huge, powerful hand holding his arm, and even though he's unaware that it belongs to a former heavyweight contender, he's still able to recognize that this request isn't an optional one.

"Sure," the young man tells him, "just let me grab my chips and - " but the man begins to pull him away from the table, telling him that there's no need to worry, the casino will take care of his winnings. "After all, we have cameras everywhere, who would steal?"

The young man is soon pushed through a doorway into a space that looks like a police interrogation room with just a single table and a couple of chairs, one of which a small, older man is sitting in. The ex-boxer wrenches the young man's arm down onto the table and holds it in place there. The young man screams as the boxer grabs a hammer with his free hand and raises it into the air, ready to bring it down on the young man's fingers.

"Well?" the old man sitting across from him asks.

The young man has started to cry a little but between whimpers he manages to ask "well what?"

The old man wants to know how the young man is cheating. No one wins the way he does, over and over, night after night, no matter the game. The young man insists that he isn't cheating, he's just lucky, he always has been, but the old man isn't buying it.

He nods to the boxer who raises the hammer up again, but still the young man doesn't admit to anything. "I'm just lucky. I'm just lucky," he keeps repeating over and over in between sobs.

The old man stands up and pats him on the shoulder. "Maybe you are," he says, before slipping something into the man's pocket. The police then enter the room and immediately take a set of loaded dice from the same pocket. He's in real trouble now.

The young man is shoved into a holding cell at the jail and looks around at the other men, wondering if his luck has finally run out.

He squeezes in on one of the benches lining the wall and accidentally bumps the man sitting next to him, waking him up from his nap. The man is angry at having been disturbed, but grows even angrier when he realizes who just woke him, it's the man who seemed to take all the luck. The young man doesn't seem to have noticed that he's upset him at all though. What he has noticed, is that there's a penny on the floor in front of him.

The young man bends to pick it up just as the man next to him throws a haymaker. His fist slams into the wall right where the young man's head just was, shattering many of the bones in his hand.

The young man jumps up with a fright and runs across the small cell as the other men being held also leap to their feet, some crying out in confusion, others cheering on the violence. The young man cries out to the guards for help but no one seems to be coming to his aid. He looks around the cell but there's nowhere for him to hide. The angry man, now madder than ever with a hand that is rapidly turning purple and blue approaches him. He lifts the young man up with his good hand, holding him in the air by his throat. "I'm going to kill you!" the man cries before the door to the cell opens. The young man watches as the TASER prongs fired by the jail guards appear on the man's chest, and he drops the young man to the floor before falling backwards from the 50,000 volts coursing through his body. The young man would learn the next day that the angry man was dead before he even hit the floor, the result of a congenital heart defect, and a lot of bad luck.

The young man stands before a judge who is listing off the charges against him, which include cheating, a felony in this state that can result in a sentence of up to five years in prison. "But this isn't your first offense, is it?" The judge asks.

The young man tries to explain that those previous times were all mistakes, he's never cheated in his life, but the judge doesn't want to hear it.

The young man is sitting in the hallway outside the courtroom when his lawyer emerges from his meeting with the judge and prosecutor.

"Boy are you a lucky guy," his lawyer tells him. He goes on to explain that even though the case against him is airtight, the charges are going to be dropped, provided he admits himself to a special program.

The young man assumes it must be some kind of gambling addiction program.

In no way is he addicted to gambling, but what choice does he have?

It's either that, or prison, the choice is easy.

As the young man exits the courthouse he is approached by a man in a suit, who leads him to a black van parked nearby. The young man is placed in the back and immediately notices that there is a cage separating the back from the front seat, like a prison transport van.

The young man is growing nervous, where are they taking him? This all seems like it's happening so fast, can it even be legal? And what about his things that were taken at the jail? "Excuse me," he asks the driver, what about my things? I don't even have my wallet.

"Don't worry about that," the man driving the van tells him. "You won't need any of that anymore.

You're a D Class now."

The man doesn't have any idea what that means, but he can tell it isn't good. His luck may have finally ran out.

The young man, who once lived the life of a professional Las Vegas gambler, was given a new name - D-87465. But as you'll see, that name wouldn't last very long, and soon would be known as SCP-181... or as the SCP Foundation staff liked to refer to him... Lucky.

SCP-181, was first noticed by the Foundation following his being arrested for repeatedly defrauding the Nevada Gaming Commission.

He was originally made a member of the Foundation's Class D personnel, the guinea pigs of the SCP Foundation who are used for various tests with anomalies in order to better understand their properties. However it soon became clear that the man's ability to consistently beat the odds had nothing to do with cheating.

In his first experiment, which took place at Armed Reliquary Containment Area-02, where he and several other Class Ds were exposed to an SCP that is known to to incite extreme anger and murderous tendencies in those who come into contact with it. Just as expected, one of the other D Class members became enraged and began rampaging, killing all of the other Class Ds present... all except for one.

Through what appeared to be a stroke of good luck, the frenzying D Class seemed to miss D-87465, who had laid down on the ground amongst the other bodies and was playing dead. An armed response team soon entered the experimentation cell and put down the rampaging D Class, sparing D-87465.

He was next submitted to a test with SCP-075, a creature that resembles a large snail with a muscular foot shaped like a six-fingered, clawed hand. SCP-075 is much heavier than its small size makes it seem like it should, weighing approximately 860 kilograms.

Despite this, it is able to move at an extremely high speed, quickly leaping towards anyone who comes near it and spraying them with a deadly corrosive liquid.

D-87465 was placed in a cell with SCP-075 as part of a test to measure its speed and reaction time, but despite SCP-075 having immediately killed all prior D Classes during tests, D-87465 somehow managed to keep avoiding its leaping attacks.

He was always able to guess which direction to move in order to dodge the deadly snail, like a soccer goalie who always picks the right way to dive to stop penalty kicks.

Having now survived not one but two experiments that exposed him to Keter class anomalies, researchers needed to find out if D-87465 was himself anomalous, or simply a statistical anomaly.

In order to test this, the D Class was placed in the containment cell of SCP-082, better known to most as Fernand the Cannibal, a grotesquely huge humanoid with ogre-like features who often dresses like a Victorian era aristocrat, and will regale his guests with outlandish stories before inevitably eating them. But there was something different about D-87465.

After a full month of survival in 082's cell, a length of time that had resulted in all the previous test subjects being consumed, SCP researchers suspected that this D Class's incredible ability to survive was much more than just dumb luck, but they needed to test him even more to see if his powers extended beyond just the ability to survive.

D-87465 was removed from regular D Class duties and researchers began performing various tests on him, watching as he flipped a coin fifty times in a row, with it coming up heads every single time. Similar results occurred when they had him roll pairs of dice that would always total up to seven, or when they had him pick random cards out of a deck and he was able to pull all thirteen hearts in a row.

Foundation researchers were now convinced that this man was more than just lucky, he seemed to possess the ability to create an unnatural effect on probability, though researchers suspected that he was generating this effect without being aware of it.

At this point, D-87465 was reclassified and given a new designation - SCP-181.

Further testing confirmed that SCP-181 is able to affect causal probability and that it really does occur through no action of his own. However there's more to SCP-181 than simply being lucky, as researchers soon found out. In an audit of death and injury rates at Bio-Research Area-12, where SCP-181 is contained, it was discovered that both had increased dramatically in the time since he was brought there. It seems that SCP-181 doesn't simply create his own good luck, he in some way saps it from others simply by being present. It now appears that every lucky moment he experiences results in the opposite happening to someone else. For every seven he rolls on a pair of dice, someone else gets snake eyes. And for every death defying escape he makes, someone else must die. There's no telling how far his ability might scale. Could he survive a nuclear blast?

And if he did, what would be the result in order to "even out" the odds so to speak.

In light of these new discoveries, SCP-181 was removed from his low level containment cell where he was allowed to occasionally interact with D Class personnel for entertainment purposes, and was moved to Site-27, where he was placed in solitary confinement and classified as Safe.

All interactions with staff are now limited to the bare minimum in order to ensure his survival and security, without risking any events that might result in him "getting lucky."

30. BOTFLY PARASITE- SCP-658

A businessman from Queens had been saving for years to get something he'd been dreaming of since childhood.

A particular wristwatch which just cost over $20,000.

However, mere days after getting his hands on the pricey accessory, he noticed a small defect on the edge of the watch case - It was a small metal nub, an imperfection that he could have sworn wasn't there when he first bought it.

After all, he paid twenty grand for the thing, surely he'd notice if something was wrong with it when he first picked it up?

He brought the watch to the official Service Center out on 5th Avenue that Friday evening.

They'd check the watch out, and have it back to him by Monday, good as new.

You don't buy a watch like this if you expect anything less than the very best.

The businessman's watch was stored in a secure vault with several hundred others as it awaited repair from a highly trained technician.

What happened next would be considered unbelievable, if it hadn't all been caught on the security camera.

The first watch began to mutate over the next eighteen hours.

It shattered into a twisted mass of glass and metal cogs, its hands shooting out in every direction as four legs and a metal eye grew out of the resulting mass.

This spider-like creature then skittered across every single other watch in the storage vault, and within another eighteen hours, they mutated too, until the room was positively alive with tiny metal creatures.

Meanwhile, over at Site-19, a guard began to notice that his standard-issue Foundation handgun was unusually uncomfortable to hold.

Perhaps he was developing a nerve issue or carpal tunnel syndrome?

It's not that uncommon in the profession.

But no, it was actually the strange metal nub forming on his pistol's grip.

He had no idea that, inside the gun, a bizarre transformation was beginning to take place.

And, within three days of the nub first appearing on the handgun, it underwent a remarkable metamorphosis.

Much like the watches, the gun mutated, growing four legs and an eye, and began running through Site-19, causing chaos.

The gun began firing with reckless abandon, sending bullets ricocheting off the walls, and injuring Dr. Jack Bright and Dr. Sophia Light as they attempted to disable the rogue pistol.

It was able to fire in a sustained fashion for over a solid minute, before stopping to synthesize new bullets through unknown means.

Eventually, the weapon was captured and subsequently destroyed for presenting an active danger to SCP Foundation personnel.

Meanwhile, in an insurance provider's office building out in South Dakota, one of the many desk drones working their fingers to the bone typing up insurance claims barely noticed a small plastic nub forming on the side of their wireless keyboard.

It remained this way for a relatively uneventful six days, before finally undergoing a complete transformation.

It became a chaotic configuration of legs and keys, spelling out the words "ASK WE WILL ANSWER" on the top of its body.

It wandered around the office, seemingly brushing up against as many other pieces of technology as it could.

The astonished workers found that if you typed any complete sentence onto this mechanical creature's keys, it would be rendered inactive for around an hour, much to the relief of everyone who was there at the time.

In New Mexico, a small child was about to be scarred for life when his brand new talking action figure developed a plastic nub on the nape of its neck.

The child didn't really pay any mind to it.

However, within ten days of the nub's appearance, the toy took on a transformation that was impossible to ignore.

The toy burst open, its head growing four legs and skittering away from its own broken body.

When the little boy saw this, he called for his mother.

When it began skittering towards him at surprising speed, he screamed and fled.

The head, which had also somehow lost its eyes to an even more frightening effect, kept repeating "Mom, there's something wrong with my toy" in the little boy's voice.

If it wasn't for the Foundation amnestics that he and his mother would later receive, he likely would have been scarred for life by the anomalous experience.

In Idaho, an old woman who lived alone noticed something strange going on with her television set, a lump of warped, bulbous plastic had started forming on the top.

She decided to call a TV repairman, or perhaps her son who didn't call her nearly enough, to come over and take a look at it.

But as things often do in life, she let it slip her mind, and two weeks passed without her addressing it.

This would prove to be a mistake - Not that any TV repairman really could have done anything to help.

The TV sprouted four long, spider-like legs, and a single eye.

The screen perpetually showed shaky footage of an unmoving figure, suspended mid-air in the middle of a blank, featureless room. This change from the usual programming disturbed the old woman greatly, even more so as the television began advancing towards her.

Meanwhile, soldiers operating a tank stationed in Syria noticed a small metal welt on its chassis.

Of course, given the natural wear and tear experienced by tanks on an active battlefield, none of them paid much mind to such a tiny defect.

It continued like this for a month and a half until tragedy finally struck in the most unexpected fashion: Much like the handgun over in Site-19, the tank grew legs and started firing in every direction, devastating nearby infrastructure and killing scores of people around it.

It seemed not to discriminate, or even really to aim.

It fired in all directions at soldiers and civilians alike, and took several groups of soldiers armed with anti-tank weaponry to finally put it down.

No explanation was ever given for what happened that day.

Most people just assumed that it was a tank operator who'd snapped under the intense pressures of war, and gone berserk, but the truth would forever elude them.

So, what is the truth?

Why has all this machinery, from innocent to disastrous, been taking on a mind of its own and causing chaos across the globe?

Allow me to explain.

These are just a few entries from the filing cabinet of incident reports belonging to SCP-658, a parasitic mechanical entity that's also known as... the Botflies.

SCP-658 instances are a unique species of highly reproductive anomalous creatures, characterized by their four long, thin legs on the underside of their bodies, and their single large, mechanical eye somewhere on the upper body.

They reproduce through contact with any man made mechanical objects, though the exact means of parasitic infection are unclear.

Simply making contact seems to be enough to turn an object into a breeding pod for a growing SCP-658 embryo and gestation time is dependent on the size and complexity of the infected object.

The embryo will present itself as a metal or plastic nub on the surface of the object, appearing to the untrained eye like some kind of minor production defect.

This keeps the embryo safe as it develops, growing and absorbing the surrounding technology into its own biomechanical makeup.

Incidentally, the name "Botfly" is a play on an equally unpleasant non-anomalous parasitic insect, latin name Oestridae, which implant their eggs into the living flesh of their victims, where they incubate, grow, and eventually burst out from the skin.

The similarities in breeding patterns of non-anomalous botflies and SCP-658 are self-evident.

These entities vary massively in size, from the diminutive stature of five millimeters squared to hundreds of meters.

The size of an SCP-658 instance, much like its aforementioned gestation period, depends entirely on its host object, and Foundation research has indicated that any complex, man-made mechanical object is susceptible to parasitic infection.

From cellphones to jumbo jets, all technology is on the table for 658.

And, as indicated through the eyewitness accounts in the case files, the appearance of the individual SCP-658 instances are reflective of whatever technology incubated them.

This influence of the host technology also appears to extend to SCP-658 behavior, with more benign objects like phones or wrist watches becoming equally benign creatures, and weapons such as firearms or combat-ready vehicles taking on a more aggressive nature.

Given that the US Military alone has thousands of vehicles and even more firearms, there are naturally some concerns about what would happen if ever an SCP-658 outbreak got out of control at a military base.

Thanks to the extreme proliferation of and dependence on technology in our modern era, a large-scale containment breach of SCP-658 could lead to a catastrophic exponential population boom.

The SCP Foundation is keeping an extremely close eye on any signs of SCP-658 activity, especially in technologically-advanced cities and other densely populated locations.

Research has proven that these creatures are capable of manifesting adaptations that increase their reproductive ability even further.

For example, during one test, it was proven that one SCP-658 instance was capable of impregnating another.

The result was it transforming into a creature with eight legs and two eyes that was capable of impregnating any objects they touched with two embryos, rather than the typical single embryo.

While senior researchers deemed it unwise to see exactly how far these 658 inter-breeding experiments could go, it stands to reason that it could also be subjected to an exponential increase.

One hyper-mutated 658 instance could be capable of mass-impregnating larger pieces of technology with hundreds if not thousands of embryos.

You can see how these often tiny and seemingly harmless creatures could quickly become a big problem for all of us.

Picture every vehicle - cars, trucks, motorcycles, scooters, ATVs, vans, humvees, tanks, planes, helicopters, speedboats, yachts, cruise ships, battleships - all becoming hyper-mutated SCP-658 instances.

Then add every phone, every laptop, every computer, every tablet, every TV, every printer, every kitchen appliance, every gun, all being infected with SCP-658 embryos and joining the horde.

Given how much all of us - including the SCP Foundation - rely on this technology and so much more in our work and daily lives, it's clear how the uncontrolled proliferation of SCP-658 would completely alter the world as we know it.

It's a clear reminder of the importance of the SCP Foundation's work: The worst-case scenarios for even some of the more innocent-seeming SCPs can be startlingly bleak.

Due to the mechanical nature of these anomalies, all connections to the Church of the Broken God and their illicit activities are being explored by Foundation field personnel.

Containment protocols on SCP-658 are extremely clear: Any instance of SCP-658 no larger than 50 CM across any axis - considered to be a "small" SCP-658 sample - is to be stored, alone, in a steel box when not being used in active testing.

Special containment procedures specify that the box must be kept closed through low-tech means, and we mean a true return to basics here: String or duct tape are the preferred methods of keeping them under lock and key, or as some researchers prefer, weighing down the lid with heavy books.

Anything with a more complex locking mechanism is capable of being impregnated by SCP-658, completely negating containment.

Any 658 samples larger than 50 centimeters are to be destroyed as soon as possible after being apprehended by Foundation personnel.

This "destroy on sight" order is also applicable for any technology infected by SCP-658 outside of intentional testing scenarios.

In order to avoid population growth during containment, all captured SCP-658 samples must be kept at least three meters away from any man-made technology capable of sustaining an SCP-658 embryo.

If unsure of whether an object is applicable, researchers and guards are told to err on the side of caution when it comes to this anomaly which has been classified as Euclid.

After all, when it comes to SCP-658 - or really, any SCPs - it's far better to be safe than sorry.

GOOD BYE AND SEE YOU AGAIN

THANK YOU FOR READING THIS BOOK!

Made in United States
North Haven, CT
07 May 2024

52250199R00113